UNINVITED

By the Author

The Universe Between Us

Uninvited

Visit us at www.boldstrokesbooks.com

UNINVITED

by

Jane C. Esther

2019

UNINVITED

ISBN 13: 978-1-63555-282-9

This Trade Paperback Original Is Published By
Bold Strokes Books, Inc.
P.O. Box 249
Valley Falls, NY 12185

First Edition: April 2019

CREDITS
EDITOR: ASHLEY TILLMAN
PRODUCTION DESIGN: STACIA SEAMAN
COVER DESIGN BY TAMMY SEIDICK

Acknowledgments

This story would never have come to fruition without the influence of my old friend Eden W., who relayed to me the legends of Seneca Lake as we spent two summers nearby in a plant pathology lab studying strawberries. Seneca Lake was home to the Haudenosaunee prior to European invasion.

Thanks to Jamie B., you know what for, you visionary genius. To Crystal Chard, you were lovely, thank you for being my beta reader. To my high school bff Jen, thank you for your insight into the diet of African grey parrots. Finally, thank you to my wife for being the understanding and supportive person I need when I'm occupied for days with a writing project.

To my biological and chosen families.

CHAPTER ONE

Aerin McLeary dipped her pale toes in the icy water of Seneca Lake. A deep, cold ache rose from the tops of her feet into her calves. She shivered, the chill moving through her like a snake.

"Zoe, aren't you coming in?" She turned to look at her best friend, who stepped backward on the grassy shore, away from the water. Zoe bounced on the balls of her feet, grimacing. It was so like Zoe to cop out at the last minute, especially when it came to cold water. To Zoe, cold was anything below eighty degrees.

Aerin shook her head and chuckled, looking out along the shoreline. The trees around them were mostly bare, reaching against the sky with deep red and early green buds. The beginning of a new season. The end of one, too.

"So, I can't convince you, can I, scaredy-cat?" Aerin already knew the answer.

"Nope, you know it's way too cold. Besides, this is your baptism, not mine." Zoe stopped bouncing for a moment and ran her gloved fingers through her long honey hair. The thin material energized the strands so she looked like a plasma ball in a science museum. "Jesus, I thought the East Coast was supposed to be warmer than Indiana," Zoe said.

Aerin chuckled. "We're in upstate New York. This is basically the snow capital of the country. I think there's a ways to go before we get to the actual coast."

"Why couldn't you have gotten divorced in July?" she whined.

Aerin rolled her eyes and stepped a tiny bit farther in, unsteadily balancing on the rocky lake bottom. She felt pressure where sharp gray stones pressed into her soles and tried not to think of Jesus on his crucifixion day. She tried not to remember the sermons that Pastor Ando had delivered over years of Sundays, Aerin in the front row for every one of them. The cold ache spread to her core and she took a deep breath, shedding the heaviness that had built up like rust, landing her here, in a freezing lake in the middle of rural New York.

"Okay," Aerin said. She relished the motion of soft waves lapping at her shins, even though she couldn't feel them anymore. "Say what you said to me before so we can get this over with and make it official."

Zoe scrunched her forehead, remembering her speech. "Okay. First you need to go deeper, or else your feet will be the only part of you that's reborn."

Aerin stumbled farther into the lake until it reached her lower thighs. She turned back to look at Zoe, her legs burning, almost numb. She accepted it as penance and scanned the shore in an effort to distract from the unbearable throbbing in her lower half. Their bright red rental convertible sat just beyond Zoe on a small road that hugged the lake, its trunk full of wine from their vineyard tours. Aerin couldn't wait to open a bottle for herself in her newly vacated home. The wind howled and blew her chestnut hair into her face, and for once, she didn't try to brush it away.

"Okay, this is as far as I can go without getting hypothermia," she yelled. She ringed the bottoms of her yoga pants around her thighs. At least she'd decided on these instead of her three-day-old jeans, which were starting to smell a bit.

Zoe cleared her throat. "Okay. My beautiful friend Aerin McLeary, have ye the strength to go forward into this life without your shit bag of a husband?"

They'd already agreed to disagree on that point. "Zoe," she warned.

Zoe crossed her arms and tutted. "Aerin, you have to listen to my words. Feel them. Be the words. Be the lake. Otherwise, this won't work."

Zoe and her flair for the dramatic, plus some new-agey witchcraft she'd recently gotten into, was a bad combination. Aerin gazed at the dull reds and dark grays of the rocks beneath the surface, trying to connect with them. What were they feeling? Her feet looked bluish from above. She hoped it was a reflection of the sky, not loss of circulation. "Fine."

Zoe continued. "To completely free yourself from the handcuffs of holy matrimony, you must pour some of that freezing lake water over your head."

Aerin stood there for a moment, a tingle fluttering down her spine. "This is not what you said before."

"Do you trust me or not? My words have power." Zoe lifted and shook her hands as if to prove the point. Aerin grumbled. This was the last time she'd agree to go along with one of Zoe's ridiculous ideas.

She closed her eyes and took a palmful of water, letting it drip onto her hair, shivering when it rolled off and dampened her shoulders.

"Good. You're almost done," Zoe said. A smile crept across her mouth and Aerin knew she was up to something. "Now put your arms out, turn five times, and sing 'I Will Survive.'"

Aerin glanced at an older couple walking their husky just

behind Zoe. They smirked when they saw Aerin in the middle of the lake, whispering something to each other that Aerin was glad she couldn't hear. Her chest tightened and she slowly let out a harsh breath, which hung in the air like a tiny cloud until it was wisped away by the wind. She didn't want to be whispered about. She never had, and that's what got her into this whole mess in the first place.

"Screw it," she said to herself. She had to stop caring what other people thought. Caring had brought her misery for too many years. Eager to be different this time, she began to do as Zoe instructed, turning in a slow circle while singing quietly. Sound carried over water, and even though she'd just vowed to be herself, there was a minimal level of decorum she wanted to maintain. As she crescendoed into the chorus, a surge of warmth slowly crept into her feet, up her calves, and through her torso. She stopped moving and looked down into the water, confused. The water was as clear as before and her feet were still a muted blue. This was probably the beginnings of hypothermia. Maybe she'd stayed in too long. Maybe she shouldn't have gone out so far. Ready to cut this ritual short, she attempted to move back to shore. To her dismay, she couldn't.

A shiver suddenly shot up her back, causing it to stiffen. Her hands were moving somehow, she could feel it, but she was unable to look down at them. When she brought them to her face, she saw her fingers were vibrating. The sensation intensified by the second. She panicked, trying once again to walk back to shore, but she remained rooted by a magnetism that drew her downward, toward the bottom. She waved her arms a little to get Zoe's attention and Zoe waved back, not understanding. How could she? Aerin didn't understand it herself.

Then a deafening noise rang out from somewhere, the sound of rusty machine components grinding against each other, of an eternally long tire skid. She felt sick, clutching at her stomach, screaming in agony, squeezing at her ears as the noise got louder and louder. It consumed her entire being until she was the sound, it was every memory she'd ever made, every thought she'd ever had. Her eardrums seemed moments from bursting and she'd accepted that she would die right here, in the middle of a cold lake in upstate New York. Then, as quickly as it had started, the ringing ceased. Aerin found herself chest deep in the frigid water, clutching her knees to her soaked sweater, tears streaming down her face. She couldn't feel anything, which was better than what she'd just felt.

In the distance, she heard yelling, but she couldn't respond. She slumped even farther into the lake, her chin skimming the surface. She felt herself slipping lower and oh, what a relief it would be to keep going, devoid of that sound, freed from the struggle to stand back up. Amidst splashing and swearing, there were hands under her armpits that lifted her dripping body from the water. She leaned heavily against a warm body and managed to take a few steps, shaking violently as the wind blew through her soaked clothes.

Together, they stumbled against the stones to shore, the water receding from Aerin's legs inch by inch. She still felt submerged, her skin swimming underneath fabric. Aerin tried opening her eyes, but her vision blurred and she started to heave, first with nausea, then with heavy, hopeless sobs.

"Aerin, can you hear me?" Zoe asked, her voice octaves higher than normal. "You're freezing, I'm getting you a blanket." Zoe made for the car, then turned back and squeezed Aerin's shoulder. "Don't move."

Aerin couldn't if she wanted to. In the distance the couple

with the husky continued walking and she was glad they hadn't noticed. She didn't like unnecessary fuss. She shivered in her soaked clothes but was otherwise intact.

"I'm going to call 9-1-1," Zoe said frantically, throwing a purple fleece blanket around Aerin's shoulders. The blanket brought her body to a painful prickling stage as it warmed her slowly. She calmed enough to notice Zoe scrambling for her phone.

Aerin shook her head, and the movement seemed make the rest of her fall back into place. "No," she whispered. She said it again louder. "Zoe, I'm okay. I'm okay." Her voice shook and she peeked at her hands. Her skin had the pallor of a week-old corpse. A massive shiver vibrated through her muscles and she felt warmer.

"I think you have hypothermia or shock or something." Zoe knelt and examined her. "Huh. Your lips are getting less purple. Your pupils look okay, actually, not that I'm an expert."

"I'm fine," she muttered.

Zoe sat back on her heels and shook her head in disbelief. "What in the world happened to you? Don't tell me you're just fine all of a sudden."

Aerin took a moment to mentally scan herself. The parts of her that had been burning with static electricity moments ago were now strong and cool with renewed blood flow. She shook her head, the one part of her that still didn't feel right.

"I really think I should call an ambulance. Whatever the hell that was, it wasn't normal." Zoe took out her phone again and began to press numbers.

"Please, no. I'm okay, I promise," Aerin said weakly. She couldn't even convince herself with that tone. "I think it was just some weird electric thing. Remember when we used to touch the Millers' electric fence for fun?"

Zoe cocked an eyebrow. Aerin should know better than

to lie to her best friend, but right now, she didn't care. She didn't need Zoe's bullshit detector on top of whatever had just happened to her.

Zoe hesitated for a moment, then asked what Aerin knew she would. "Are you saying this because you're actually okay, or because of what people are saying about you back home?"

With the words out in the open, disgust hot as lava surged through her. She knew what her neighbors in Tireville, Indiana, said about her. She was too good for one of the town's beloved sons? She must have something wrong with her head. She certainly didn't have the authority to practice therapy, especially her godless brand. She could never live down yet another example of mental instability.

"Because I'm okay." It was a lie. She somehow stopped her tears to prove her point. A light breeze dried the traces of salt to her cheeks, which were strangely warm. She was glad her body was cooperating with her ruse. "Maybe we can go back to the hotel and I can lie down for a bit."

She must have looked worse than she felt because Zoe didn't take her gaze from her. It was penetrating, trying to catch her in the lie. "Would you rather start home tonight?" Zoe asked.

As much as she hated the idea of ending their vacation early, Aerin found herself nodding. They still had a couple more days planned for Aerin's Marriage is History Tour, Zoe's brilliant term for their Finger Lakes winery vacation, but the ill effects migrated around the inside of her body, now as a giant, pounding headache.

"Okay, let's get you a shower and some dry clothes." Zoe unlocked the doors and helped Aerin slide into the seat. She put the top up and blasted the heat, not taking her eyes off Aerin until they were required for the road.

CHAPTER TWO

Olivia sped down the highway in her WRX, weaving in and out of traffic. The engine purred as she hit eighty-five and she relaxed into the supple leather seat. She didn't have time to sit behind a bunch of Sunday drivers, for some reason on the road this Friday night. She had a date and Ben was certainly already waiting for her.

She skidded into a space at the edge of a crowded lot in front of McGillicuddy's Bar & Grill and hopped out onto the gravel. As she closed the door, she noticed a fine white scratch glaring against the blue paint, just below the handle. Damn. When had that happened? She'd have to remember to buff that out later.

Inside, Ben Stevens waved to her from a table near the back, flashing his megawatt smile in her direction. She waved back and weaved through the mostly full tables, bumping into at least two chairs before sliding in across from him. A gaudy red and green light fixture hung so low between them that they both, being on the taller side, had to peer around it to see each other.

"I ordered you a drink already. Your usual. Fry?" Ben asked in his deep baritone.

Olivia reached for the basket. "You're the best. Thanks, buddy. Haven't seen you in a while. How's life?"

Ben arched his back and stretched against the red vinyl of their booth before resting his arm along the back. "Really good. I think Jody told you I have a new girlfriend," he said, smiling.

She thought about it for a moment, fishing for a conversation she couldn't recall. Girlfriend…girlfriend. Nope. "Yeah, she did mention that. Tell me more." She stuffed another couple fries into her mouth.

"Not too much to tell just yet. I met her on a dating app and we've been on a couple dates so far. The second one lasted three days." He smirked. "I like her. She's hilarious, and she's so attractive you might even be interested." Olivia smiled and watched his eyes light up as he chuckled to himself. She hadn't seen him this happy in a while and certainly not over a relationship.

She lifted her hand in the air to high-five him. Their palms met in a satisfying crack and they grinned at each other. "So, I do have to ask, why are you hanging out with me on a Friday night instead of your new girlfriend? This could be the beginning of a two-day, three-night date, am I right?"

Ben considered it for a moment, then nodded.

Olivia continued. "I mean, don't get me wrong. I'm flattered, but whenever I date someone, I'll at least bring them to the bar with me." Though when she tried to remember the last time she'd actually brought anyone anywhere, she couldn't. Since Daria, she hadn't really dated at all.

Ben knew as much and smiled as he checked his phone. "She's actually coming back early from a road trip she went on with her best friend. I'm talking like, best friend from childhood. Isn't that crazy? I don't have any childhood friends."

Olivia shrugged.

"Anyway, they just crossed into Indiana. Oh, I was going to run something by you."

Olivia raised her eyebrows. "Yeah?"

"Something weird happened to her friend and she was hoping you'd take a look for her, at least on the brain side of things."

Her curiosity fizzled. People didn't seem to understand that when she got her PhD, she became a researcher, not a medical professional. Ben should know, though, she thought, bewildered. "That's what neurologists are for. I'm definitely not qualified to do a casual assessment of 'something weird' that happened to her friend's brain," she said, using air quotes to their fullest extent.

Ben shrugged. "Yeah, I don't know. It seems like her friend wanted to keep things on the down-low for some reason. No doctors. No records."

"That sounds extremely sketchy. And anyway, it's a little more complicated than looking her over, if we're going to run tests. I'd have to get her signed on to a study, which I don't have running at the moment. Otherwise, there'd be all sorts of liability issues."

Ben mulled her words for a moment. "Don't you have some kind of equipment in your house? Would it have to go through the IRB if you aren't using the university's facilities?"

Oh, he was playing that card. She had, after all, collected the old lab equipment so she could run off-the-record experiments on herself and her friends. And the groundbreaking work she performed on Mr. Piddles, her parrot, had produced some surprising results. She sighed for effect. "I mean, it still should go through the IRB, but I see where you're going with this," she said.

"I'm not trying to pressure you, but I know how you roll. You can't pass up a good mystery." His eyes sparkled. "Shall I let her know you'll at least do a baseline EEG on her friend?"

Olivia flipped her hand and pretended to look at her nails. "Fine, but make it next weekend. Send my address. If she turns out to be a weirdo, or if I get in trouble somehow, I'm blaming you."

Ben put his hands in the air. "Got it."

Olivia guffawed and swatted his arms. "Put your hands down. You're making this look like a holdup." She chuckled.

"Big black man being held up by a skinny-ass Asian woman. Yeah, I'm sure that's what it looks like. Besides, I don't have anything for you to steal."

Olivia withdrew. "Hey, don't look at me. I don't pay your salary. Get yourself a nice, juicy grant and you'll be set for life. Okay, not life, but at least a few months." Olivia remembered being the broke grad student trying to make ends meet. She'd been living in Chicago and she'd had to take odd jobs here and there. She'd also lived with Daria, and as dysfunctional as the relationship was, it helped defray some of the financial burden. At least in Indianapolis, housing was cheap enough for Ben to have his own apartment.

"What do you think I used to spend Friday nights doing?" Ben asked.

"It'll happen, bud. You're doing good research and somebody wants to fund the next step. Plus, Dr. Winslow will give you a good recommendation for your postdoc when it comes to that."

Ben nodded and they sat in silence, sipping their drinks. Olivia had nothing but respect for Ben and his work in biochemistry. He had to work twice as hard to find half the opportunities as his white colleagues did. Olivia benefited from the Asian genius narrative, but she had short hair and presented, she thought, as obviously queer. In the Midwest, not exactly a picnic.

"So, what about you?" Ben asked, wrenching her from her thoughts.

"What about me?"

"You haven't dated anyone in a while. Aren't you going a little stir-crazy?"

Olivia frowned. "Nah, I don't really have time for it." Actually, she was tired of looking. Nobody could hold her interest for more than a few days. There was only one person who ever had, and it was long past time for Olivia to get over it. That relationship ended half a lifetime ago.

"Between this project that I'm working on and the study I'm doing with Mr. Piddles, I'm spent. No time for love," she muttered, playing it off as no big deal.

"You'll find someone. You're the coolest lady-loving lady I know," Ben said. His eyes twinkled with admiration.

"Thanks. How's your dad doing?"

Ben frowned and looked at his hands. "He's recovering okay, I guess. My mom took it pretty hard. She spends a couple hours at church every day when the nurse is at the house."

Olivia winced at the mention of church. She couldn't help it. Somewhere out there, her father wielded his influence as a pastor to spew hate to his Baptist congregants. Somewhere, he was hijacking someone else's life, and for what? For power? For some fucked-up image of a malevolent God? After years of contemplating, Olivia still hadn't figured it out.

"Er, sorry. I know how you feel about churches," he said.

"No, no, I asked."

They sat in a comfortable silence for a while. Ben didn't ask about her family because he knew she had little to speak of. Grandparents she rarely spoke to, a mother she talked to once a year on Christmas. Oh, and a little brother she hadn't even met. It was no skin off her back. Her colleague, Jody, had turned out to be an incredible big sister-slash-parental figure and she had other friends that she considered family.

"What's happening on *Sunrise Lane*?" Ben asked after a while.

Olivia looked up at him with a smirk. "Master of distraction. I know you don't really care, but I'll tell you anyway, since you asked."

Ben sat patiently as Olivia recapped the last month's worth of episodes, which she watched religiously every night. Davis had risen from the dead and Paige realized she still loved him. Oliver killed his grandmother for her money and had escaped, living in Paige's house to avoid detection. Sandra was rumored to be interested in both Tom and Toni, the very attractive fraternal twins who had only met each other last year. "So, the usual," she said. "Lots of drama so that I can live vicariously through other people and not have to engage in my own." Her gaze fell to the table and a pit formed in her stomach as she swallowed the lie. She wanted the drama, the ups and downs, but didn't know how to find it anymore. The bitterness and longing that she'd held on to for years crept to the surface.

"Last fry?" he asked. A peace offering, making up for something he'd said that Olivia didn't even blame him for.

"Sure." She chewed it slowly to savor the empty comfort. She did her best never to dwell on the past, but sometimes it seemed impossible. When she got like this, pulled under by the heavy weight of memories, sleep provided her only refuge.

Finally, she said, "Hey, it was good to see you tonight. I should go home and feed Mr. P before he gets mad."

Ben nodded. "Let's do this again soon. I'll send you a text

with whatever Zoe tells me about her friend and when she can come over."

Olivia froze at the name, her heart skipping a beat. The only Zoe she knew of was the one who'd befriended Aerin right after Olivia had been kicked out for being gay. Of course her reaction was ridiculous and she quickly shook it off. It was just a name.

She thanked Ben and headed out to her car, a mysterious shadow of dread hanging over her as she made her way home.

Chapter Three

A erin felt a soft blow to her shoulder and heard someone calling her name. It sounded far away and muted, as if resonating through a thick wall of glass. She struggled to open her eyes, but they didn't budge.

"Aerin? Aerin, we're home. If you don't wake up, I'm going to have to drive you to the hospital."

Images of the county hospital with its whitewashed walls and pale blue linoleum appeared in her mind. Half the town worked there and they talked to the other half. Her mother, the head nurse, would make sure the entire staff was on Aerin's case. Rumors would spread like wildfire through Tireville, burning down everything Aerin held dear. The few things still standing, that is. She couldn't let that happen.

With all of her strength, she lifted her heavy eyelids, blinking against the darkness. Her small brown ranch house stood before her, its windows shimmering with the pathway lights she'd installed before the trip. She hated the idea of coming home to darkness, even as she relished being alone. She could only handle so much change at once and she'd about reached her limit before she stepped into the lake.

"Hmm," said Zoe.

"What?"

"Look." She swiveled in the driver's seat, pausing to take Aerin's forearms. "You're stubborn and that's one reason I love you, but you shouldn't put your life in danger because some assholes want to ruin your reputation. Can't we at least call Meg?"

Every inch of Aerin wanted to protest, but exhaustion kept her voice low. "I'll make you a deal. You stay with me tonight, and if I'm not better by tomorrow, you can call Mom." She yawned deeply.

Zoe scrunched her forehead, then nodded. "Fine. Let's get you to bed."

Aerin lay on her queen-sized bed for what felt like hours, staring at the ceiling and running through all of the mental exercises she could think of. In between counting and reciting the alphabet backward, she decided there wasn't anything wrong with her. The lake incident had scared her, nothing more. She drifted off sometime after, relieved that she was completely, 100 percent okay.

In the middle of the night, Aerin awoke to the sound of someone tripping over the table in the hallway.

"Shit. Goddamnit. Why is this table still in the middle of the hallway? How many times did I tell her to move it? Does she listen?"

Aerin got up and cracked open the bedroom door. "You okay out here?"

Zoe shrieked and backed into the small table again, releasing another chain of swear words.

"It's just me," Aerin said, chuckling. The hallway seemed brighter than usual, the small night-light glowing with extra vigor. Must be a side effect of waking up during a dream.

Zoe rubbed her hip and met Aerin at the door, reaching out to touch her arm. Aerin's skin prickled at the sensation and she shivered. "I'm sorry for waking you up. I just had to get my phone and then this frickin' table, seriously?"

Aerin crossed her arms and smirked. "I like my table right where it is."

"You suck. So, what, are you awake now? It's pretty late. Or early. Whatever, it's the middle of the night. You should probably get some more sleep."

Aerin shrugged, realizing she didn't feel tired at all. "I'm a little hungry, actually."

"Okay, let's get a snack. I actually had an idea that I wanted to discuss with you."

Aerin prepared two peanut butter sandwiches and mixed some powdered lemonade in a pair of glasses. The cloud of sour pink dust from the jar burned her nose and made her cough. She brought the food over to the round kitchen table illuminated by a small chandelier on its dimmest setting. She took a bite of the soft bread with its gooey center as soon as she sat down on one of her red vinyl chairs. It tasted heavenly, as if she'd never entertained her taste buds with the salty, earthy flavor of peanuts before. How could this one peanut butter sandwich stand so far above the thousand others she'd had in her lifetime? By the time Zoe had chewed and swallowed her own first bite, Aerin was licking the peanut butter off her fingers.

"Hungry much?" Zoe stared at her, no doubt noticing how Aerin's gaze kept flicking back to the counter where the sandwich materials beckoned.

"I'm just going to…"

Zoe nodded, her wide eyes on Aerin as she made two more sandwiches, extra peanut butter. Aerin blushed as she sat back down at the table and scarfed both of them down as quickly as the first.

"Jesus."

"I don't know. I'm starving." On a good day one sandwich would have been her limit. Tonight she was three in with room for more. Her heart pounded as she watched Zoe eat, hyperaware of every movement her friend made, each arch of her eyebrow as her expression changed. She couldn't unfocus, and for the first time since the lake incident, she acknowledged that maybe its effects had indeed lingered.

"So, I was thinking," Zoe said slowly.

Aerin sucked in a deep breath.

"Look, you can totally ignore the idea if you want. Just forget I ever said anything." She hesitated.

"Zoe, you haven't said anything yet. What is it? Just tell me. If I hate it, I'll just kick you out of my house."

Zoe put her hands over Aerin's arm and squeezed. "I think you should talk to Olivia about this," she said in a rush, then cringed as she waited for Aerin's response.

At the mention of Olivia's name, Aerin's spirit sank. Her stomach swirled with old, bitter emotions. She sat back in her chair, pulling her arm away from Zoe's touch, shaking her head.

"What does Olivia have to do with anything?" What an inopportune time to bring up her one regret, the person she'd hurt more than anyone, even her ex-husband. The reason she'd married him in the first place. She couldn't see how Olivia could possibly help her and besides, she didn't plan on seeing Olivia ever again. They'd both made mistakes and that bridge had burned long ago.

"Well, you know that I've been dating Ben, right?" Zoe asked. Aerin nodded. "Well, he works in a lab at the university down in the city and Olivia works there, too, in the same building. His boss is kind of like her mentor. They're all friends. He says Olivia's really chill."

"If you say so. I haven't exactly kept in touch with her." Aerin folded her hands and played with her fingernails, fighting the intrigue. "She's a researcher?"

"Full professor, actually. Apparently she's the hot new thing at UI. She does some kind of brain science. Anyway, Ben hangs out with her sometimes and if you refuse to go to a doctor, maybe you could at least talk to Olivia. Maybe she can help somehow."

Aerin shook her head. "I don't think she'd want to see me. Plus, you don't even know if she can help."

"So, you admit you do need help." Zoe crossed her arms and leaned back in her chair with a satisfied grin.

"Hey, no fair. Anyway, she probably still hates me, and I don't blame her. Do you not remember what happened?" Aerin mostly tried not to remember the awful and cringeworthy things she'd done, but living in Tireville, she couldn't escape them completely.

Zoe sighed. "I remember. Not your best moment, but people change. You've basically come full circle." She winked at Aerin, who narrowed her eyes.

An image of Olivia's terrified face flashed in her mind. The face she'd made when Pastor Ando had walked in on them in his church. The face she'd run out on without a second look. "No. I can't ask her for anything. Try again, Einstein. Any other brilliant ideas?"

"So, again, don't hate me."

"Zoe."

Zoe grinned and opened the messages on her phone, flashing the screen in Aerin's face. "She's agreed to see you. Isn't that great?"

Aerin's head whirled and she felt a swell of anxiety in her stomach. This could not be happening. "No. That is not great. Does she know she's agreed to see me?"

"Well, I called Ben while we were at a rest stop yesterday to see if he had any ideas. I guess Ben's boss suggested Olivia. As for whether she knows it's you, I'm not entirely sure. Ben just told her it was his 'girlfriend's friend.'"

Aerin tried to process the myriad feelings that bubbled to the surface from deep inside. "I'm not going," she said.

Zoe pleaded with her eyes. "This could be good for you, especially now." Aerin knew what Zoe meant, though she didn't agree that she needed this kind of coming out party.

She stared at the table and took a deep breath. This couldn't be the answer, could it? She hadn't seen Olivia in something like fifteen years. She'd carefully avoided her on social media, scared to find that she'd be happy, terrified that she wouldn't be. "Look, there are a lot of feelings there, for both of us. I take the blame for screwing up the most and there's no way I'm dredging that up. I honestly hope I never see Olivia Ando ever again."

CHAPTER FOUR

Lunch had just let out into third grade recess and Aerin's stomach was full of cafeteria cheese pizza and Cheez Doodles. While the rest of her class ran around the giant wooden play structure, she kicked at the gravel and slowly walked the perimeter. She didn't know most of her classmates yet and she was secretly scared to go into the playground because of the bees. Last week she saw Jenny Conway get stung by a bee that lived between two boards of the structure. The welt on her arm still hadn't disappeared.

It was a hot September day and a bead of sweat trickled down her back. She neared the back edge of the gravel, bordered by a hayfield. A gawky stick of girl swayed alone on a rubber swing. Aerin had passed her in the hallway a few times but didn't know her name. The ponytail that tamed the girl's hair had come loose, messy wisps flying back and forth with every movement of the swing.

The girl looked lonely, not in a pathetic way, but like she had already exhausted her options for interesting interactions with her peers. Aerin took a deep breath. This was perfect. She needed a friend who wouldn't make fun of her when she talked with a funny Pittsburgh accent. Maybe she would even be charmed by it. Aerin made her way over and sat on a swing at the end of the set, moving side to side slowly, kicking at the gravel. The girl stopped swinging and instinctively stiffened. Aerin smiled to lighten the mood. The girl glanced at her warily, staring and then looking away, then staring again. She wore a tie-dyed T-shirt, possibly the prettiest thing Aerin had ever seen with its bright red, orange, and yellow swirls. She'd always wanted a shirt like that.

In the distance a group of loud boys played touch football. Aerin watched the girl scowl in their direction and decided for sure that they'd be friends.

"Hi, I'm Aerin. What's your name?"

"Olivia." The girl hesitated slightly. "Are you new?"

Aerin nodded. "Yeah. I've been here for two and a half weeks so far. We moved because my mom got a job at the hospital."

"Oh," Olivia said.

"My dad wasn't really treating her right, so we had to get out of there. The houses here are cheap and so is the gas," Aerin said, repeating what her mom had told her countless times, excuses for moving deeper into the middle of nowhere. She didn't really care about gas or house prices, but she thought it made her sound smart.

Olivia nodded, her face lightening for a moment. Good. It had impressed her new friend.

She moved swings so she was next to Olivia and began to swivel side to side. "What class are you in?"

"Mrs. Hansen's. She's pretty nice. She calls on me a lot," said Olivia.

Aerin knit her eyebrows. She hated being called on, even though she usually knew the answer. She didn't want to mess up in front of her new class. "What do your parents do?"

Olivia shrugged. "My dad is the pastor at the Baptist church and my mom does laundry and cooks."

"That's neat. My mom usually works during dinner, so I have to eat leftovers or go to the neighbor's," Aerin said, looking at her shoes.

"You can have dinner at my house if you want. My mom always says there's room at the table for anyone in need."

Aerin didn't know how to feel about that assessment, but it seemed innocent enough. "Okay. You can ask her if I can come."

Olivia nodded, now looking fully at Aerin, studying the wavy hair that fell all the way down her back. Aerin liked the feeling of Olivia's eyes on her. It made her feel welcomed and it would make her mom happy. She'd been harping on Aerin to make at least one friend per week. If Olivia turned out to be her best friend, wouldn't that count as two, to cover the two weeks that had gone by?

Just then, the bell rang and recess ended. They both groaned and flopped against the swing chains, laughing at their identical reactions. The rest of the kids also took their time getting back up to the school, where they'd form lines by class and march back into the rest of their afternoons.

She and Olivia slowly made their way toward the parking lot. Neither of them were ready to part ways. "Hey, I'm having a birthday party next weekend, do you want to come?" Aerin asked.

"Okay. I mean, are you sure?" Olivia looked dubious, like she'd been tricked by this line before.

"Of course. You're my new best friend," Aerin said, smiling. She ran ahead to meet her class, turning once to wave at Olivia, who just watched her, beaming.

CHAPTER FIVE

Five minutes after three, Olivia huffed at her empty living room. "Seriously? I'm donating my afternoon to you, random friend of a friend with a brain issue, and you can't even show up on time?"

She glanced out the living room window again, but the street was empty. Maybe Ben had given one of them the wrong time. She groaned dramatically. There were so many other things she could be doing, like watching a movie with Mr. Piddles. He always had the most entertaining commentary, especially if she chose a horror film. He had a spot-on bloodcurdling scream and somehow always knew when the characters were about to be attacked or murdered. She considered letting him out of his room to admonish her tardy guest, but he was a mean old bird and she didn't feel like consoling a crying stranger.

She turned to the window again as a beige sedan pulled up in front of her house. Finally, she thought. She couldn't see much of the driver, but what she did see piqued her interest. It looked like she'd be meeting with a semi-attractive woman around her own age. Poor choice of car, but she could look past that. The driver cut the engine and gingerly stepped out. Nice hair, Olivia thought, as its brown waves blew lightly in the wind. The woman turned toward the house and noticed Olivia staring. She gave a shy smile and waved. Olivia instinctively stepped backward, away from the window, clutching her stomach. She felt as though she'd been punched.

The footfalls on her front steps brought her back to an awful reality. Time seemed to slow down and fade away. Olivia's head spun as she tried to make sense of the fact that an unmistakably older Aerin McLeary stood outside her door, knocking lightly. She wanted to run into her bedroom and hide, maybe scream into her pillow or something juvenile like that.

No. She did not agree to help the woman who so easily and exquisitely tore her heart in two and then tossed her like an empty can all those years ago. She stood frozen in front of the door, unable to bring herself to open it, unwilling to confront feelings she'd buried deep inside that she hoped would never resurface. Aerin knocked again and Olivia gulped hard, her hand reaching out to the doorknob of its own volition.

She opened the door a few inches and blinked at the sight in front of her. Yup, still Aerin. She meant to shut the door in Aerin's face, but instead swung it wide open and stood aside. Aerin gave her an uncertain smile and walked inside as though Olivia had invited her.

"Thanks for agreeing to see me," Aerin said as she slipped her shoes off. Habit, Olivia thought. Olivia never asked any of her guests to remove their shoes, but her mother sure had.

"I didn't," Olivia said, her voice strained.

Aerin's face fell. "You didn't know it was me." She took a deep breath and nodded. "I wasn't sure, but I was hoping you had a heads up."

"Nope." Olivia studied Aerin's face, which objectively looked more beautiful than it had the last time she'd seen her. It did not fool Olivia, though. She knew Aerin's deep penchant for betrayal.

"I can go, if you want." Aerin pointed her thumb at the door and shifted her weight in its direction.

She wanted more than anything to agree, to see Aerin walk out the door forever and forget about her all over again, but there would be no forgetting her now. Really, there had never been. Olivia sighed at the vulnerability in Aerin's eyes. Call it morbid curiosity and self-inflicted torture, but she wanted to find out what in the world prompted this little reunion.

"No, you can stay," she said, her hands on her hips, anchoring her to that decision.

Aerin nodded and glanced around the room. "You still have that language book," she said, reaching for conversation.

Olivia nodded and wondered why she did still have it. Aerin had given it to her on her thirteenth birthday after Olivia had declared she would be a Spanish interpreter when she grew up. For some reason she'd kept it, though she couldn't remember the last time she'd taken it from the shelf.

Aerin glanced at her and started to say something, but stopped herself. A mournful look flashed across her face. It bore a distressing similarity to the one she'd thrown Olivia fifteen years ago when they'd last seen each other. In the middle of their junior year, Olivia's father had walked in on them doing ungodly things in a house of God, his house of God, and her whole world had blown up. She'd been sent away and Aerin had reacted by becoming the perfect little Baptist in Martin Ando's congregation, or so she'd heard.

The memory crippled her, sending pangs of panic into her chest. She had to figure out how to bury it again, keep the regret to a minimum.

Olivia cleared her throat and gestured toward the kitchen. "Can I get you something to drink?"

There had been a time when Aerin would have made herself at home, grabbing her own glass and rifling through the cupboards to find whatever junk food Olivia's parents had hidden. The lack of familiarity was almost as unsettling as Aerin being there in the first place.

"Water would be great."

Olivia nodded and they moved to the kitchen. She watched Aerin carefully pull out a barstool and hop on. She looked really good. Maturity had served her well. Of course it had. Olivia hadn't been there to distract her with lesbianism and naïve lust. Aerin had the perfect straight kind of life that her father preached about. As she turned away to fill the glasses, her eyes filled with tears. She quickly blinked them away and handed Aerin the water.

"Thanks," Aerin said as she took the glass. "You have a nice place."

Olivia nodded. "I've done pretty well. I bought this house when I got the position at the University of Indiana a few years ago."

"Right, congratulations. I hear you're a hotshot brain researcher. Which brings us to why I'm here," Aerin said uncertainly. They looked at each other for a long moment.

"Olivia! Olivia! Come here!"

Aerin jumped at the shrill noise and spilled water on the front of her navy infinity scarf. "Is that—"

"Mr. Piddles. Alive and well."

Olivia followed Aerin as she raced into the guest room toward the noise.

"Mr. Piddles, I didn't think I'd ever see you again," Aerin exclaimed. She trudged through the newspapers on the floor and over to his perch, reaching her hand to pat him on the head.

"I hate you," Mr. Piddles said at the first touch. "I hate you, you're an asshole. You're an asshole."

Aerin dropped her hand, dumbfounded. Olivia burned

with embarrassment, imploring the grey parrot to stop his tirade with a pointed stare.

Aerin's eyes widened and she stepped away. "Um, I guess he remembers me."

"Sorry, he's very smart. Smarter than most parrots. He remembers a lot," Olivia said meekly. She didn't tell Aerin that Mr. Piddles heard her say those words recently, as part of her experiments, of course. Unfortunately for Aerin, an old picture of her had made it into a pile of photos that she asked Mr. Piddles to analyze. She may have given him a hint on that particular analysis.

Mr. Piddles continued squawking and leaning toward Aerin, dipping his head back and forth. "You broke my heart. You broke my heart. You broke my heart." She definitely had not taught him that line. He must have pieced it together himself by watching *Sunrise Lane* and adding context. Fascinating.

Olivia saw the tears welling in Aerin's eyes and remembered that she could look into his interesting sentence creation later. She backed out of the room and prayed Aerin would follow her.

"So, the equipment is in the basement." Olivia inched down the hall.

Aerin shuffled from the room and closed the door behind her as fast as she could. She leaned against the wall with a sign of relief. "That was awkward."

"Yup. Probably best to get started with the EEG," Olivia said. Your own fault, she thought wickedly.

They descended into the brightly lit basement, its walls a pale gray that completed the lab like feeling of the space. Olivia breathed in the familiar smell of isopropyl alcohol mixed with a staleness that had been left by the previous owners. She'd haphazardly gathered used testing equipment over the last few years and had amassed quite a supply. If she wanted to do some of her more radical side projects, she couldn't rely on her usual funding streams.

"This is it." She stood by as Aerin surveyed the room.

"Huh. This is like one of those medical torture rooms from medieval times, updated for the twenty-first century." Aerin laughed nervously and walked around the tangle of wires and machinery, careful to avoid getting too close. "What kind of shady things are you doing down here?"

Olivia shrugged. "I wouldn't say shady, exactly. Just not completely, 100 percent allowed at the university. Couldn't get funding for some of the stuff I do down here."

To Olivia's surprise, Aerin started chuckling.

"What?" she asked.

Aerin shook her head. "You have not changed one bit."

Olivia felt herself pale. How dare she? "I have," Olivia said bitterly. "I've changed a lot since…since I saw you last."

"Maybe on the outside, but you're still the same at your core."

Olivia huffed, annoyed at Aerin's casual assessment of her life. She knew nothing about Olivia anymore and she'd guaranteed that she never would with the way she'd left things. "Well, so are you, which is why we should get this over with and then you can go back to your husband and the happy little life you've built for yourself."

Aerin's eyebrows shot up, but she didn't say anything. Good, she'd hit a nerve. Olivia gestured for her to sit in a leather chair next to a computer monitor, and squeezed a gel solution onto her hand. As she worked the gel into Aerin's scalp, she tried to tell herself this was no different than all of the other people she'd hooked up to an EEG over the years. But it was light-years away. This was Aerin, here again, her gorgeous chestnut hair beneath her fingers. Olivia had dreamt about and dreaded this moment.

As she attached the electrodes, she mumbled her usual spiel about how they would work and what the output should look like. Aerin didn't say anything, just nodded and stared at her hands. The first brain waves that showed up on the screen jumped all over the place, denser and more erratic than what she'd expect to see in a healthy human brain.

"Can you take a deep breath and try to relax?" Olivia asked.

She heard Aerin fill her lungs and let the air out with force, but the results still showed a higher rate of brain activity than normal. They were the kind of results she'd expect to see from a person having a seizure. She shut the machine off, alarmed.

"It looks like there's something wrong with the readout. It actually seems like you're having constant seizures," Olivia said.

Aerin's eyes went wide. "I'm not having seizures, am I?"

Olivia took a flashlight pen and shone it in Aerin's eyes, then had her follow the pen up and down, side to side. "I don't think so, but there's no way your brain is functioning with normal activity right now, unless something here is broken." Aerin's eyes went wide. "The equipment, I mean."

"I don't understand. What does it look like, exactly?"

Olivia considered hiding the shockingly heavy activity from Aerin, but it was her brain, after all, and she deserved to know. She turned her laptop around and leaned against the large arm of the chair.

"Okay." Aerin glanced across the screen. "I don't get it. What's it supposed to look like?"

Olivia brought up another window and opened two files. "These are normal EEGs." She scrolled through them, pointing out moments of increased activity to Aerin.

"So, mine is bad, right? I mean, I don't feel like my brain is racing or anything."

Olivia turned toward Aerin and took a deep breath. "I don't think we can say anything conclusive yet. It might be a machine malfunction, so I'll have to tinker with it." Against her better judgment, she did actually want to get to the bottom of this, especially if it had to do with broken equipment. And to do that, she needed more information. Olivia sighed. She'd done what she'd promised, but without context, the test was useless. "Do you want to go upstairs and tell me what happened to you?"

Aerin looked at her as if it were some sort of trap, but nodded anyway. "Yeah. That would be good." As their eyes met, Olivia remembered how disarming Aerin's had always been. After all this time, they still had the same effect, coaxing her deeper. A sudden thought threw her off guard. Maybe there were layers to the pain she'd carried with her all these years, only one of them hatred.

Upstairs, Aerin toweled the gel out of her hair as she sat across the kitchen island from Olivia. She cradled her water glass like a transparent shield. "Zoe and I were in the Finger Lakes in upstate New York on a wine tour, a little over a week ago. We stopped by a beach for a thing Zoe wanted me to do and I was in the water doing the thing she told me to do." Aerin averted her eyes and blushed.

"A thing. Okay. I won't ask." Olivia assumed this thing involved nudity. Aerin, naked in a lake. Not an image she needed to see at this particular moment.

"So, I was in the cold water and suddenly I felt this crazy fire-like burning that started in my toes and moved up my body kind of like this." Aerin drew her finger from her foot, up her sides, and toward her throat. Olivia followed it, awkwardly tracing Aerin's body with her eyes.

"I don't even know how to describe it." Aerin thought for a moment. "Like, you know when you touch water so hot it feels cold?" Olivia nodded. "Kind of like that. My spine was tingling like crazy. So, then I felt this vibration inside my head that turned into this loud noise, like when someone puts a mic too close to an amp, mixed with nails on a chalkboard. It kept getting louder and I couldn't tell if it was coming from inside me or outside and I assumed everyone else would be able to hear it, but apparently nobody did. It was horrible." Aerin's eyes teared up as she recounted the events.

Olivia studied her for a moment. It did sound like some kind of neurological glitch, the only external explanation she could think of being electrocution, but that didn't fit. The loud noise threw her off. She mentally crossed electrocution off the short list of possibilities and cleared her throat. "What do you think it was?" she asked.

Aerin shook her head as if that would give her some clue. "I don't know. It sounds crazy, but since then, I've been really hungry, even though I've lost a couple of pounds."

"How hungry?" Olivia asked.

Aerin bit her lip as if she were deciding how much she should reveal. "Like, I ate three eggs, six pancakes, and half a package of bacon this morning for breakfast. I ate two granola bars on the way over. And I'm starting to get hungry again."

"Jesus," Olivia muttered. "So, your metabolism is in high gear, likely caused by the insane amount of activity in your brain. That's the technical term for it, by the way." Aerin's face lightened a shade and Olivia chuckled to herself, glad Aerin was able to find some humor in the situation.

"So, the key here is, what actually triggered it?" Olivia asked herself. She felt more comfortable in investigator mode than she did as a person who remembered Aerin as the girl who broke her heart. She could work with this, even though she hadn't agreed to do more than take a baseline assessment.

Ben knew her too well and had guessed that she'd want to solve the mystery no matter the circumstances. Bastard.

Aerin hunched her shoulders, defeated, and Olivia sighed. "I guess you better come back so we can try to get to the bottom of what's going on with your brain."

She perked up and searched Olivia's face. "Do you mean that?"

Olivia nodded curtly.

"Thanks, I appreciate it. I would go to a regular doctor, or talk to my mom, but I can't, for reasons I don't really want to discuss," Aerin said.

Olivia hadn't thought about Aerin's mom in years and suddenly she missed her. Meg McLeary had been nothing but wonderful, even as she'd probably guessed that Olivia and her daughter were sleeping together. The thought of talking to Meg felt like a warm hug, but too much time had passed for her to reach out now. The distance between them stretched in many directions.

She turned her attention back to Aerin. "Maybe next time you can tell me the reasons you can't talk to your own mom about this."

Aerin gave a weak smile. "Maybe."

CHAPTER SIX

Olivia rolled out of bed at the first vibration of her phone alarm. Her head pounded and she tried to remember if she'd ended up sleeping at all. She rubbed her hands against her face to wipe some of the tiredness away, but her body felt heavy and slow. Aerin waltzing back into her life had affected her in a big, obnoxious way.

Sometimes she really wished she had a job where she could easily call out sick. She had too much to do today, too many students to meet with, a class to teach, and a lab to oversee. She slogged through her morning routine, perking up a little when she took Mr. Piddles out of his cage to eat his morning birdseed. He sat on her shoulder, chattering away, as she checked her work email and sipped bitter black coffee that didn't work nearly fast enough. Her usual plain yogurt was an easy way to start every morning, function over form. She'd eat some oatmeal when she got to work and had her morning chat with Jody.

Despite her exhaustion, Olivia managed to leave fifteen minutes earlier than usual. She arrived at the university way ahead of rush hour, before most of the other professors in her department had even left for work. Esmeralda, the building's supervisor, tinkered with the security system behind the tinted glass doors as Olivia stepped through. She waved as she went by, too tired to engage. Her oxfords made squeaking noises on the brown linoleum floors as she walked to her office.

Strewn across her desk were photocopies of journal articles. A stack of student papers peeked from a manila folder, waiting to be graded. Olivia dropped her messenger bag on the floor and sank into the cushion of the decadent faux leather chair behind her desk, a gift from her department after she'd been granted tenure earlier this year. She glanced impassively around the small room at her numerous awards hanging in tacky black frames next to a bulletin board with the covers of every renowned journal in which she'd published. There were twenty, an impressive number for such a young researcher and Olivia knew she should be proud. Lately, they had begun to seem like someone else's achievements.

She'd banked her happiness on her prestige and, somewhere along the way, had realized that while all of her research ultimately helped other people, it had failed her. Her Holy Grail, creating the world's first brain-computer program that could decipher a person's true emotional intentions, seemed like an insignificant and silly goal, more a product of her dramatic youth than her intelligence.

She heard Jody's heavy footfalls in the hallway and crept from her office, sneaking down the hall and into Jody's office right after her.

"Jody," Olivia said, inches behind her best friend.

"Holy Christ," Jody answered in her deep Texas twang, swinging around with her hand over her mouth. "Olivia, you know I scare easy."

"I do."

"So, don't do that." Jody scowled, smacking her on the shoulder.

Olivia chuckled. "Noted. Hey, so I wanted to talk to you about something."

Jody nodded, rifling through her large Coach bag and pulling out two instant oatmeal packets. "You owe me. Go make this and then we can talk."

Olivia happily swiped the packets from Jody's hand, returning moments later with two paper coffee cups full of steaming oatmeal.

Jody warmed her hands with the post-microwave heat. "Thanks. Cold out there today." She adjusted her frameless glasses and looked at Olivia curiously.

Olivia blew on a hot spoonful of oatmeal and caught Jody staring. "What?"

"You look different. Did something happen this weekend?" She leaned in conspiratorially. "Did you finally meet someone?"

Well, that couldn't be further from the truth. Olivia chuckled and shook her head. "Is it really that easy to read me?"

Jody squeezed her arm and smiled, her gray eyes twinkling. "Hon, I just know you too well. And yeah, you're pretty easy to read. So? Which was it? Hot date or terrible tragedy? You've had this same look on your face for both."

Olivia felt the small amount of joy from her prank dissipate. She cleared her throat, unsure where to begin. "I guess I should start by showing you this." She took out her phone and pulled up a screenshot of Aerin's EEG.

Jody's eyes went wide and she said, "Oh, they're glitching real bad."

"I told you not to call it that," Olivia said with amusement. Jody, a computer scientist, used her computer science words to describe everything about Olivia's work with brains.

"Okay, well, that's clear epilepsy. Is this from someone

who's a vegetable now? Because there's no way that much overload can mean anything good for a person."

"No, she's very much alive and not seizing. Looks like you can't pass this one off as a 'brain is equivalent to computer' scenario, can you?" Olivia kept her grin in check. It was an argument they had often. Jody believed that brains were simply really efficient and evolved computers. Olivia disagreed, at least vocally. She hated to imagine she was just a bunch of bits and code. Though if humans were just glorified computers, that really made everything a lot easier for her as a researcher. She just had to figure out the correct input and output.

"Hey, I didn't say that. Brains can be rebuilt, just like computers. You've seen the work they're doing at Stanford with those amnesiac war veterans. Still sticking to my theory." Jody raised a smug eyebrow and leaned back with crossed arms. "Who is that from, anyway? Or are you not allowed to tell?"

Olivia considered not answering Jody's question, but they didn't keep secrets from each other.

"It's an old friend." She shrugged. That seemed like a happy medium between telling the truth and not having to get into it on a Monday morning.

Jody stood and planted her fists on the desk, leaning over so far that Olivia could see the shadow of her cleavage. "Holy Christ. I can see right through you, woman. It's her, isn't it?"

"Jesus, Jody. How the hell do you do it?"

Jody sat down, a smirk on her face. "Ben might have mentioned he sent someone named Aerin to you this weekend." She waited for a moment as Olivia narrowed her eyes. "I might have suggested he talk to you in the first place."

"Jody."

"Even if I hadn't known those tiny details, nothing knocks

Dr. Olivia Ando off her horse, so I knew it had to be real good. Also, you told me about Aerin a couple times, remember?"

Olivia blew out a breath and pinched the bridge of her nose. She did have a nasty habit of bringing up Aerin when she was drunk.

Jody continued. "Anyway, I know you're still hung up on her, and the opportunity presented itself, so I thought it might be good for you to get some closure."

"I am not." But even as she said it, she thought about the emotional roller coaster she'd been riding ever since the weekend. If she were truly over Aerin, she wouldn't feel that way, would she? Olivia felt her face heat up in anger.

"And I am obviously right, by that look on your face."

Olivia grabbed a piece of scrap paper from Jody's desk, crumpled it, and hurled it at her. "You suck, you know that?"

Jody ignored her and patiently tossed the paper ball into the recycling. "So? How was it, seeing Aerin again?"

Olivia hadn't really figured that out and she didn't think anything other than some good, solid sleep could help her put the pieces together. "It was not what I imagined. I mean, not that I imagined it. You know what I mean."

Jody smirked. Sometimes her friend could be maddening, but she was irreplaceable, a sort of stand-in for Olivia's absent parents. Sometimes she even gave good advice. A moment of silence passed between them, Olivia staring at her hands and Jody watching her struggle with feelings she couldn't quite make out.

Finally, Jody spoke. "Why don't you get some more readings from her? See if this one was your machine or her brain."

Painfully extricating herself from the emotions that muddled this investigation, Dr. Ando the researcher slipped back. "That's what I was thinking. I already invited her back.

But what if it's the same? She doesn't want to see a psychiatrist or neurologist for some reason. It's just me. I'm not really sure I'm equipped to handle something like this. I'm not a doctor," she said. Jody arched a brow. "You know what I mean. Not that kind of a doctor."

Olivia could feel her heart starting to race, and she struggled to calm herself down from this uncharacteristic panic. She'd only spent an hour with Aerin, but its effects had spread into last night's sleeplessness and this morning's anxiety. Olivia just wanted to go back to before the weekend, before she knew what it would feel like to be in the same room as Aerin again.

"So, we'll deal with that as it comes. Get her one of those portable EEGs and get some more data, then we'll look at it together. Brains equal computers, remember?" Jody said.

Olivia rolled her eyes, unwilling to show her gratitude for Jody's wisdom. "Have to get to my first class. Thanks for the chat, Doc."

"Anytime, Doc," Jody called as Olivia left the room.

When she got back to her office, she saw a text come through from a number she didn't recognize. *Thanks for seeing me yesterday. Let me know when I should come by again.*

Just like that, Olivia's already fissured world collapsed into dust.

CHAPTER SEVEN

That night, Olivia called Mr. Piddles to the basement, where he hopped onto his special swing and bobbed his head from side to side.

"Good boy," Olivia cooed, stroking his soft gray feathers.

"More," he said in a voice similar to hers when she stopped to get a treat. She grinned and repeated the motion. He'd do this until she told him they were done. If it were up to the parrot, she'd be petting him all the time.

"Are you ready for your lesson, sweetie?" Olivia touched her nose to his beak. "You're very handsome today."

"Teach me, Mom," he said, following it with a whistle. Her heart swelled and she gave him a little peck on the beak.

"Okay, buddy. Today we're going to have you look at pictures of people and tell me what they're feeling. First, you have to take your pill." She held the white capsule out to him, and with some hesitation, he grabbed it, crushing it in his beak.

"It never tastes good, Olivia," he said. She knew this from the countless other times she'd given him the supplement and he'd said the same thing. Frowning sympathetically, she stroked his head again and give him a freeze-dried mealworm treat. The compound might not be pleasant, but it greatly increased the speed at which he picked up new language and concepts.

Over the years, she'd tried a number of supplements, mixtures, and combinations, and this seemed the most promising.

Olivia hoped that someday she'd be able to publish a study on parrot cognition with supplemental enhancement. Groundbreaking research, applicable to unlocking human potential that futurists had only dreamed about, but PETA would be all over her for experimenting on her pet. Those fuckers killed puppies, though, so she had little patience for their opinions.

Aerin, however, was a human subject, one who would potentially consent to a study if Olivia could make some headway helping her. She had a few hurdles to overcome, namely figuring out what the hell happened to Aerin and then replicating it, and that was aside from the questionable ethics of using an ex-girlfriend as a research subject. If she could figure out all those little things, she could trade her parrot in for a human subject. And if the results mirrored what she'd seen with Mr. P, it would be Nobel-level research.

"Olivia, pay attention to me," Mr. Piddles said in a high-pitched voice. She snapped out of her thoughts and settled on his beady eyes.

"Sorry, pumpkin. Time for your helmet," she said, fastening a tiny metal contraption lined with electrodes to the bird's head. She'd made it from the spoon of a ladle and glued the sensors on. It was the cheapest and most effective piece of lab equipment she'd ever owned.

"Fire me up!" he squawked, and stepped from side to side in excitement.

Olivia pulled up a slideshow of faces on the computer and turned on a video camera. A stock photo of a blond woman smiling appeared on the screen.

"The woman is happy." He whistled a few times.

"Why?" Olivia asked.

"She sees something beautiful. Like a rose or sunrise."

Olivia chuckled. Surely he was referring to the opening credits of *Sunrise Lane*.

"Good. What about this one?" She advanced the slide to a man with a disgusted look on his face.

"He ate something bad."

"What did he eat?" she asked.

"Give me a kiss." He leaned toward her and made a smooching noise.

Olivia shook her head. "No, that's for after, and you know that."

They went through the series of pictures and Mr. Piddles correctly identified most of the expressions, plus the reasoning behind them. Olivia remotely programmed his television upstairs to play the usual string of soap operas so he could strengthen his reasoning skills. She always gave him homework to do, and besides, he loved *Sunrise Lane* as much as she did. Maybe someday they could have a conversation about it.

"We're done for tonight. I'll give you a kiss now and we'll do this again on Tuesday, okay?"

Mr. Piddles responded by touching his beak to her nose and making a kissing noise. "I love you," he said.

"I love you, too."

He jumped down from his perch and spread his gray wings before half flying, half jumping up the basement stairs. Olivia smiled and remembered the first time she'd met him, decades ago. An older congregant at her father's church had fallen ill and ended up in a nursing home; Olivia had jumped at the chance to take the bird. She'd trained him from the start and he'd been there during the confusing, wonderful, dark days of her teens like nobody else had.

She owed him everything, treated him like the queen's corgis, and gave him mostly free rein of the house when she was home. She'd even built an outdoor enclosure attached to a window so he could spend time there in the summer. Besides companionship, he served as a research subject without the years of baggage that humans brought with them.

But humans it would be, ultimately, if she wanted to make a real impact. Now that she had one with a brain anomaly to study, she might finally be able to do that. Why did it have to be Aerin?

Chapter Eight

A erin closed her laptop and leaned back in her creaky secondhand office chair, stretching her arms. She'd been on chat therapy calls since noon and couldn't wait to see her first flesh and blood client of the day. It was exhausting trying to read someone's expressions when they had an archaic internet connection and their face kept freezing up. She tried to be excited that her burgeoning therapy practice finally brought in some new patients, but today, she was just going through the motions, waiting for Olivia to respond to the text she'd sent two days ago. She couldn't blame her for the silence. She'd need years of therapy herself to unravel the convoluted web between them.

She glanced at the clock on the wall, its plastic face catching the glare from the mid-afternoon sun. Her gaze latched onto the second hand ticking in its arc, jerking forward and sometimes slightly backward before pulling ahead again. The motion enthralled her in a molasses haze kind of way. She felt her thoughts slow, then fly away altogether, and could almost taste the emptiness between the movements. The ticking grew louder, until it was the only sound in the room, pulsing in her ears. Tick, tick, tick. She felt herself stand and walk to the other side of the small office, closer and closer to the clock, inches away, then millimeters, forehead against the plastic. Her face twitched, ticking with the clock. It felt pure, she could see the space between the ticks, and it was vast. Between them was an emptiness that stretched forever.

She stayed there for far too long, pressed up against the clock, until someone knocked on the door. Abruptly, she stepped backward and realized what she'd done. The clock read 3:04, four minutes past the appointment time.

"Mr. Bingham? Sorry, I was just finishing up some paperwork. Come on back," she called, catching her breath as she stumbled back to her desk.

The smell of cigarette smoke preceded Mr. Bingham and Aerin tried not to gag. A middle-aged man with graying hair and sunken eyes walked into the room with a slight limp.

"Welcome. Have a seat," she said.

"Hi," he said gruffly. He adjusted his faded jeans and work coat as he sat on the navy love seat she'd bought secondhand. The fabric was so dark, you could barely see the pilling on the arms.

"Make yourself comfortable. Can I get you some water?" She picked up a pencil and a pad of yellow-lined paper from the desk, which she hated. The clunky gray and white finish on the desk felt more used car salesman than inviting therapy practice, but it was free from Zoe's bank branch when they'd done a reorganization. She could afford free.

She began to tap the pencil against the paper as she walked to her seat near Mr. Bingham. Somewhere along the way she stopped walking and stood, tap, tap, tap, drawing her in like the ticking of seconds. She noticed before Mr. Bingham seemed to, and before she lost too much time.

"I don't need water," he finally said. After a moment, Aerin remembered asking the question he was answering.

A few silent minutes into their appointment, Aerin could

tell it would be like pulling teeth to get this guy to open up. "So, do you want to tell me a little about why you're here?" She flipped the cover of the steno pad and wrote the date and what he'd told her on the phone. *Arthur Bingham. Going through divorce. Symptoms of depression.*

"Well, my wife left me," he said in a husky murmur.

Aerin nodded. "How does that make you feel?"

"Like garbage."

"Let's start from the beginning."

Arthur told her how he and his wife had met and that she'd transferred to a different school district once they separated. "I'm still working in maintenance at Sillington. Haven't seen Susan in weeks. Usually, I just go home and watch TV, have a few beers, pass out on the couch."

Okay, maybe they were going to get somewhere after all.

"Arthur, can you tell me a bit about why she decided to leave you?"

Arthur gave a few half answers, amounting to his wife losing interest in him. She concentrated on his face while taking notes, hardly looking at the pad. Writing legibly without looking down was one of her gifts.

"So, your wife left you because she got tired of seeing you? Because you're unattractive?" She had a feeling there must be more to the story and could see it in his eyes, the way he hesitated and looked to her left for just a moment before he met her gaze. Arthur was hiding something.

He cleared his throat and reached for the tissue box, which made a hollow, empty sound as he dropped it on the coffee table.

"I'm sorry, I didn't notice. Let me get you another box." She closed the cover of her steno pad and placed it on the edge of her chair, pencil on top. As soon as Aerin stood to reach for the box on her desk, both pencil and pad fell to the floor.

Aerin grabbed the box and turned back toward Arthur, who bent to retrieve the fallen objects. As he picked up the pencil, he looked up at her, horrified. Aerin scrunched her brow in confusion, then glanced at the notepad, which ended up halfway under her chair. The page that still stuck out into the room had just three words pressed in dark graphite, as if she'd traced the letters over and over. *Sex with student.*

Arthur stood and put his hands on his hips, shifting uncomfortably. His upper lip glistened with perspiration. Aerin's jaw dropped as she looked from the paper to Arthur and back again.

"Where'd you hear that?" he growled, leaning toward her until his figure loomed over hers. "Where'd you hear that? Somebody call you?"

Aerin slid back against her desk, clutching the edge as she slowly moved toward the door.

"Mr. Bingham, please calm down. Nobody called me."

"Then why'd you write that? Huh?" His eyes were wild with anger and fear, and Aerin could somehow hear him in her head, screaming in frustration. He wanted to run, or hurt her and then run. He wasn't sure which, and she didn't want to find out.

Her voice shook. "Mr. Bingham. Arthur. Arthur, I can help you. I just need you to calm down, take a breath." She could feel his fear as if it were her own, her forehead damp and her palms sweaty. Her pulse beat hard in her neck. She wanted to slip into it, let herself listen to the pauses between heartbeats, but Arthur's confusion sank in her stomach like a pit.

She heard a faint noise, a slight ringing in her ear, and didn't recognize it at first. An alarm going off in the hallway? Arthur didn't seem to notice, his eyes darting back and forth between her and the door. Suddenly, the sound seemed to burst from its confines, blaring into her ears like a thousand horns.

She gripped her head and collapsed into a squat, unable to take the weight of the noise as it pierced and muddled. Then, as quickly as it had started, silence.

Arthur stepped back and put his hands up as if to protect himself from whatever hex Aerin had just placed on him. She let out the breath she'd been holding and shuffled to the other side of her desk, never taking her eyes from Arthur, who inched toward the door.

"You've got nothing," he said with disgust. "Nothing." He flung the door open so hard that if it had been heavier, the knob would have left a dent in the wall. Aerin listened as his quick footsteps faded down the hall and down the stairs. Once he'd left the building, a sob escaped her covered mouth.

"Jesus. Jesus. Jesus." It was partially prayer and partially an exorcism of the tears she didn't want to cry. "You're okay. You're okay." She took a few deep breaths and began to feel a little better. Her hands shook violently as she picked up her cell phone to call the police.

"Stop." She willed her hands into stillness. While the dispatcher connected her to the police, she recalled the words on the pad. It didn't make any sense. How had she known?

"Did he confess the incident to you?" the officer asked as he took her story.

"Yes," she said without thinking. He had, in a way. She hoped they would take her word against his. After all, it was the word of a licensed therapist against that of a custodian. Not exactly fair, but that was how the cookie crumbled in this country.

When the call ended, Aerin whimpered into her fists. She wrung her hands and tried to make sense of what had just happened. To occupy herself while she waited for the police to arrive, she checked her email over and over, refreshing for mail that didn't arrive. She finally sent a quick email to Zoe, who wouldn't check it until she got home. Aerin would have a little time to collect herself before the inevitable hysterical call.

Her feet tapped a quick rhythm against the thin beige carpet as she distracted herself from what she really wanted to do: call Olivia. A little because of the brain stuff and a little because she just wanted to. They certainly weren't at that level of friendship now, but they had been once upon a time. Before Aerin turned her back on the person who had always been there for her at times like these. The fault wasn't completely her own, but she could have tried harder. She could have at least reached out in the years since. She resolved not to be that person anymore, too guilty and afraid to make amends. New and improved Aerin would own her mistakes and learn from them. Olivia would want to know what had just happened, and even if she didn't, Aerin wouldn't apologize for wanting to tell her.

She opened the short text conversation she'd started with Olivia and typed. *Call me as soon as you can.*

CHAPTER NINE

A *erin it's me. Call me please.*

Aerin leaned against her locker in the high school's main hallway, fingering the torn-out notebook page. The short message had been slipped between the grates earlier that day. It had landed on top of her history textbook, folded in quarters, and she'd only seen it as she gathered her homework at the last bell.

She read the note again, her stomach churning with an unidentifiable mixture of emotion. No way could she call. She'd been avoiding Olivia for the last few days, making sure she took bathroom breaks when her best friend had class at the other end of school, leaving as soon as the bell rang.

No, she really shouldn't call. Talking to Olivia on the phone, hearing her confident, sweet voice would be torture, so she crumpled the note and stuffed it deep into her backpack. The history book crushed it against the bottom of the fabric with a satisfying crunch. She walked at a quick clip down the hallway and took the shortcut home to her small yellow house on the edge of a wheat field. She owed Olivia an explanation, but first, she'd have to figure out exactly what for.

In her room, Aerin started her evening ritual of self-hatred.

She took off her shirt and bra and stood in front of a full-length mirror. She made a disgusted face, partly for fun, and partly because she was unhappy. There were bulges in places there shouldn't be, flatness where she wanted form. Her mother always told her she looked healthy, but Aerin didn't believe her. She was fat and ugly, plain and simple.

"No, you're just a teenager with a poor body image. I'm a nurse. The head nurse," she would remind Aerin. Meg McLeary was the expert, end of discussion. Aerin would nod and pretend to agree, but she knew, deep down, that nobody wanted her.

At least, she was 100 percent sure of that until last weekend, when Olivia had whispered, "I think you're pretty," into her ear, her breath tickling Aerin's neck. They'd been watching *Titanic* at Aerin's house for the twentieth time and Aerin had casually mentioned that she wanted to be as pretty as Kate Winslet someday. *I think you're pretty.* She heard the words over and over, had suddenly noticed the way Olivia's elbow rested on the pile of pillows between them. The way her hair draped over her shoulder and glowed with the muted browns and blues of the movie. Aerin had closed her eyes and inhaled the buttery popcorn haze that hung in the living room like a cloud. She tried to focus on the familiar dialogue of the movie, but she only heard her own heartbeat, heavy in her chest, and Olivia's soft laughter. Later, once Olivia's mom picked her up, Aerin ran to her room and burst into tears. She couldn't pinpoint the reason, only that it included a twisting feeling of loss.

Aerin tried not to think about the *Titanic* incident as she put on a loose tee and a some parrot print pajama pants, a birthday gift from Olivia. She made her usual dinner of boxed macaroni and cheese, stirring the cheese powder into the macaroni for so long that she barely registered the phone ringing. Her mom sometimes called around dinner to check in, so without looking at the incoming number, she picked it up.

"Hello?"

"Hi," said a voice decidedly younger than her mom's. Her stomach lurched. "Did you get my note?" Olivia asked.

Aerin hesitated. "Uh, yeah. I was going to call you in a little bit."

"Well, don't you want to know the good news?" Olivia asked.

Aerin relaxed a bit at their ongoing joke. "Is Jesus going to save me?"

"Praise be," Olivia said, laughing. They both considered organized religion a waste of time, not to mention a patriarchal cesspool that only functioned to erase women's lives. Aerin would never have come up with anything so radical on her own, but she agreed wholeheartedly with Olivia's assessment.

Of course, Olivia had to attend every service, and Aerin showed up as a matter of tradition. If you weren't a churchgoing person in Tireville, people talked about you. Besides, it gave the two of them something to make fun of.

"Remember how I was going to ask my dad if youth group could do an overnight camp this summer?"

"Yeah," Aerin said.

Olivia continued with excitement. "He said yes, but it's going to be super Jesus-y and I need you to come with me so I don't have to share my tent with a serious Bible freak. Please?"

Aerin's heart slammed into her throat. Sharing a tent with Olivia. She gulped. What could she do? Say no and miss out on an adventure with her best friend? Condemn her to sharing a tent with someone who wouldn't properly appreciate all that Olivia Ando had to offer? Or say yes and torture herself with feelings that were probably not real and definitely not right?

Sleeping next to Olivia in the confines of a dark tent, their breath mingling in the damp air, terrified and tempted her.

"I kind of already signed us both up," Olivia blurted. Aerin's heart stopped for a moment and she inhaled sharply. "Sorry, I should have asked you first."

She sighed, relieved in a way. The decision had been made for her. She would go on a camping trip with her best friend and she would pretend she wasn't in love with her.

"Aerin, are you there?"

Aerin pinched the bridge of her nose. "Yeah, yeah, I'm here. I'll go, since you signed me up."

"Is everything okay? I haven't seen you since the last time we watched *Titanic*. I miss you," Olivia said gently.

"I miss you, too," Aerin said automatically. The words surprised her as they came out, but they were true. "I'll see you tomorrow at school."

She hung up the phone and felt a longing for Olivia that she was sure would never go away.

CHAPTER TEN

Olivia's office hours couldn't end soon enough. She had a constant stream of students in and out, confused about what she wanted them to do in their three-part finals project. She understood their confusion, annoying as it was to explain the assignment over and over. Jody told her she taught like she thought, fast and deliberate, sometimes a little dense for the undergrads who weren't expecting so much material. Though Olivia had earned a reputation as a hard-ass professor, students were lined up around the block to secure a place in her lab and her lectures were always full. She didn't worry about making them work hard for their grades.

Her phone buzzed against her desk and she picked it up, assuming Jody was texting about dinner plans. When she saw Aerin's name on the screen, she put it right back down, wincing as she slowly picked it back up. She'd agreed to help Aerin out, and to do that, she had to stop avoiding her. Finally, she read the text and groaned. Why couldn't Ben have sent literally anyone else to her for help?

Aerin picked up immediately when she called, a little out of breath. "Thanks for getting back to me right away."

"No problem. What's going on?"

Aerin hesitated a moment. "There was an incident at my

office and the police are coming by any minute. I just, I thought you should know." Her breath came hard and fast through the phone, and Olivia's skin prickled with goose bumps. An incident?

"Aerin, what happened? Are you okay? Did it have something to do with your brain?"

"Yeah, I think so. I'm okay. I ended up pissing off one of my clients and I'm pretty sure he was going to hurt me." Aerin sniffled and blew out a breath. "I'm okay."

Clients? She recalled Ben mentioning something about his girlfriend's best friend being a therapist but hadn't put the pieces together. It all made so much sense. She probably had so much of her own shit to work through that she would make a good, even great, therapist. She shook away the momentary bitterness, ashamed of herself for demeaning therapists. She only meant to hurt Aerin.

"Jesus. He didn't do anything to you, right?" Olivia asked softly.

"No, I'm a little shaken up but okay. I think I picked up on a thought he was having and then wrote it down. Like telepathy, I guess."

Olivia's heart sped up and she pressed the phone closer to her ear. "You can read minds?"

"I don't know. I guess? I wrote something down that he definitely didn't say. When he saw it, he flipped out."

"What was it?" Olivia asked.

"He had sex with a child. A high school student," she whispered.

Olivia's eyes went wide. "Oh, wow. Holy shit. But you just wrote that down from his thoughts? That's incredible." Somehow, Aerin's brain had leveled up. Olivia had long believed that telepathy was possible if enough synapses were firing at the same time. This would allow the person to access the network between everything in the universe, which was, according to her, what some people called God. Olivia imagined it as a giant web, constantly making connections and passing along information. Aerin could be her proof, if she figured out how her brain had become unlocked.

"It's not incredible, it's disgusting. It was terrifying and he almost killed me. He definitely thought about it for a moment," Aerin said, her voice shaking.

Olivia stood and leaned against her desk, pinching the bridge of her nose. "Yeah, right, I'm sorry. Look, I think you should come by my office soon so we can run some more tests."

Even if she couldn't define her feelings toward Aerin, she knew she was onto something with the telepathy. If she could somehow translate the mechanism behind it into computer software, she would be that much closer to building the program that would decipher emotions, the program that could have helped her avoid getting involved with Aerin at all. It seemed fitting that Aerin should be the means to that end.

Olivia heard a noise on the other end of the phone.

"Oh, I think the police are here. Can I call you later?" Aerin asked.

Olivia didn't want to put the phone down before they'd set a time to meet. She didn't trust herself to pick it back up if Aerin rang. "Actually, do you want to come by the university tomorrow so I can set you up with an EEG headset? I'll text you the address. If you have time, that is."

Aerin's tone lightened. "Thanks, Olivia. I can come by."

She hung up and leaned back in her chair, regarding her walls impassively. Her chest tightened with nervousness over their next meeting. Her feelings were all over the place. She pushed it out of her mind and thought about what really mattered, the science, the discovery. If her partnership with Aerin could survive, there would be many more papers to add to the bulletin board. And if she could take it a step further, she might be able to bring her research with Mr. Piddles into the mainstream.

CHAPTER ELEVEN

Olivia got up at 6:45 on the dot every day, never one to consider sleeping in. So, as she half-consciously hit the snooze button that morning, reveling in the feeling of Aerin's arms around her, she knew she was officially fucked.

She couldn't help it. Dream Aerin and her sensual burnt sugar body lotion held her hand, smiled at her, had embraced her for so long that Olivia woke up feeling a comfort she hadn't known in ages. At the second alarm nine minutes later, she finally opened her eyes. She knew Mr. Piddles would be waiting for her, but she wanted to make this last. Reality would never be this good again. She closed her eyes and saw Dream Aerin's beautiful face and the amazing smile that made Olivia want to be friends with her in the first place.

They had been as close as two friends could be until that night camping in the woods with Jesus, as they called it. And then they were more than friends for a year and a half and their relationship had been magical, messy, and beautiful. She was sure they'd never be apart, until the moment they suddenly were. Olivia's father had walked in on them in the sixth row of the Tireville Baptist Church, probably half-clothed and mid-moan. She'd blocked out the details in self-preservation.

Martin had just stood there, dumbfounded. Looking at or through them, Olivia hadn't been sure.

Later, after her father had moved past the initial shock and long past the time when Aerin had run out of the church and left Olivia alone with him, Martin Ando made up his mind. He sent Olivia to live with her maternal grandparents in Chicago. They were not religious and therefore were as close to hell as his daughter. Then he set his sights on the one person he could easily mold into a perfect Baptist. Aerin, suddenly worried about her reputation, quickly turned a one-eighty. At least that's what Olivia heard from mutual friends, with whom she'd later lose touch. For Martin, it was the perfect redemption, a way to keep the situation under wraps while gaining a devoted follower. Olivia could never forgive either of them for this betrayal.

And then Aerin showed up out of the blue. While Olivia apparently still reeled from the heartbreak, her body remembered the good times. She was thoroughly turned on and going to be late for work. This would have to wait for another day.

"Fucking idiot," she mumbled. "Of course she still turns you on. She's still attractive and you still have working eyes." Probably more attractive than before, she thought, an inconsequential truth. Adult Aerin had confidence beyond what teenage Aerin would have thought possible. Adult Aerin was also happily married, to a man. That last realization sobered her up and propelled her out of bed. Aerin could only be a brain to her, a research subject, she reminded herself. A person who had the potential to make her very, very famous.

Olivia got to work a little later than usual and hurried to Jody's office, where she found a mug of oatmeal waiting for her. Jody casually leaned back in her chair with a self-satisfied grin.

"You're never late," she said.

"I'm not late. It's basically the end of the semester." Olivia took a big spoonful of warm oatmeal and let it slide down her throat.

"Oh, sweet Olivia. You know I can tell when something's up. So, what's up?"

"Nothing," she said quickly between bites.

"Nothing? Really? Did you eat anything this morning?" Jody asked, narrowing her eyes and giving Olivia a good once-over.

Olivia huffed and slammed the oatmeal down on the desk, splattering a little on the oak finish. "Goddammit, Perralta. Doesn't your husband get tired of your constant questioning?"

Jody chuckled, her eyes lighting up as she looked across her desk. "He knows better than to keep secrets from me."

Olivia shook her head. "I have no secrets."

"I'll get it out of you one way or another. You know that, right? I have my ways." Jody leaned back in her chair and tapped her fingers together.

"If your ways are hooking me up to some electrodes and running my new neuron model with your software, then you'll be very sorry to hear that it's not working correctly yet. Anyway, it's really nothing and I have to get going because I'm meeting Ben to help him out with a grant application this morning." Olivia stood to leave. "Lunch in a couple hours?"

Jody winked. "You know it. I'll meet you at your office."

While she usually loved spending time with Ben, Olivia's meeting with him that morning seemed interminable. She kept checking her watch and glancing at the door, waiting for Aerin to walk in at any moment. She should have given her a specific time. Ben finally noticed she was paying more attention to the time than to him and rescheduled the rest of their meeting.

"Oh, by the way, did you ever get in touch with Zoe's friend?" Ben asked as he gathered his things.

"Yeah, I did," Olivia said in an accusatory tone.

Ben went wide-eyed. "Oh, did it not go well?"

"Well, you neglected to tell me exactly who was coming." Olivia played with a pencil and avoided Ben's gaze.

"Sorry, I didn't realize it mattered."

Poor Ben. He had no idea and it wasn't his fault, really. Olivia just wanted someone to blame for the pit in her stomach as she waited for Aerin.

"Nah, sorry I brought it up. It's actually completely fine. I just knew her when we were kids, that's all."

"That's great. I bet you had a good time catching up." Ben smiled uncertainly.

Olivia nodded. "Yup," she said with a completely straight face. She didn't have time to explain anything more to Ben now. Aerin could be there at any second.

After he left, Olivia busied herself with some edits to a paper she'd received back from peer review. One of the researchers attempting to replicate her experiment had been unable to get past one step, a really easy one. The mistake was certainly his, but Olivia couldn't pinpoint it. Funny how the reviewers with the most critiques were always the older white male researchers who didn't realize she made sure her methods were bulletproof before sending the papers out. She couldn't afford mistakes.

By lunchtime, still no Aerin, and Olivia wanted to jump out of her skin. Jody popped her head around the door. "You ready?"

"Uh, yeah, let me get my stuff." Olivia stood, flustered, and knocked a pile of papers to the floor.

"My, my. A little off today, aren't we?" Jody smirked as she bent to help clean up the mess.

"These are daggers I'm shooting at you with my eyes. I hope you can feel them." Olivia glared. She felt off-kilter, terrified by the way Aerin had turned her life upside down in a matter of days.

To her surprise, Jody hugged her. "Look, I don't know what's gotten into you today, but it looks like you need this."

Olivia squeezed back and nodded. "Yeah, just a little worked up. Thanks. Let's get out of here." As much as they teased each other, Jody kept her grounded like nobody else.

They got halfway down the hall when Olivia slowed and stopped, staring straight ahead. Jody noticed right away.

"Oh, so I was right. That's what's got you all tongue-tied and in a tizzy. That must be Aerin," she said a little too loudly.

"Shh, don't yell, she'll hear you." Olivia watched as Aerin looked down another corridor, then recognized her and waved.

"You've got it bad, don't you?"

Olivia gave her a small shove and felt her cheeks color. She certainly did not have it bad, and the intimate scenario that played out in her dreams had definitely not been real. So why did she have the urge to put her arms around Aerin when she approached?

"Hey," Aerin said, her voice shy and quiet like a soft wave over Olivia's body. She wore an orange sweater with a bright yellow infinity scarf that gave her ensemble the air of a beautiful torch. Jesus, that dream really did her in.

"Hi." Olivia kept her hands firmly by her sides. "Jody, this is Aerin."

"Aerin, it's great to finally meet you." Jody extended her hand as Olivia glared at her. "I think I'll run to lunch and leave you two alone. I'll bring you back something, Olivia. Aerin? Anything for you?"

They both shook their heads at the same time, Aerin to

answer the question and Olivia to admonish Jody for even suggesting such a thing. Sharing food with the ex was not in the plan today.

"Great, see you later. Nice to meet you, Aerin," Jody said over her shoulder.

Olivia watched her walk away and wished she hadn't left so soon. She turned back toward Aerin. "So, find the building okay?"

"Yeah, it was exactly where it said it was on the map. Don't get down to the city much anymore, but plenty of parking here, which is nice." Aerin looked at her with an expression that mirrored her own. This small talk was weird. They'd gone through far too much together to discuss stupid, mundane shit like this.

With a nod in the direction of her office, Olivia led Aerin down the hall. She did her best to stay slightly in front so she wouldn't have to look at Aerin's devastatingly attractive outfit. Aerin had always excelled at fashion. Olivia had grown into her slightly androgynous style, but Aerin, ever the looker, had somehow become even sexier and more feminine in the last decade and a half. Olivia told herself to cut it out with these thoughts. Aerin wasn't hers to lust after.

"How are you doing after your brush with the maniac?" Olivia asked, facing forward.

"Not bad. I pretty much moved on right away, which is strange for me. You know how I like to dwell on things." Olivia furrowed her brow. She didn't know anything about what Aerin liked or didn't like anymore. To her credit, Aerin noticed her assumption and blushed. "Right, anyway, it's like every time I start to remember how terrified I was, I just tell myself to stop being upset about it. And then I stop," she said.

"Did he get arrested?"

Aerin half laughed. "If he hasn't already, he definitely will. Statutory rape is not something the police take very lightly."

"Good point."

"Yeah. I had to give the cops my statement after you called. Let me tell you, showing the Tireville Police your creepy, overly traced pencil marks really makes you seem like just another hometown girl."

Olivia chuckled and unlocked the door to her office, holding it open for Aerin to pass. She caught a whiff of body lotion that smelled strangely like the burnt sugar scent in her dream and automatically closed her eyes for a moment, remembering.

Aerin gazed around the room, noticing all of Olivia's framed awards. Olivia watched her, suddenly proud of her work, a feeling she thought had been lost to her early career. Her phone vibrated and she tore her eyes away from Aerin. A text from Jody.

You had good taste.

Olivia immediately swiped the message away, blushing, and resumed watching Aerin admire her work.

"You've done well. Congrats." Aerin looked at Olivia with wonder. It felt good, being looked at like that. Just like the old days.

Olivia crumbled under the scrutiny. "Thanks. I've been busy. Have a seat." She looked Aerin over and noticed that she shone with a glow that she hadn't had a couple weeks ago. "Have you lost weight? You look…vibrant is the only word that comes to mind."

Aerin shrugged. "I guess. I wasn't trying to lose weight. In fact, I can't stop eating and I'm still losing weight."

"Oh, I'm sorry. That's terrible."

"You said it was 'vibrant,' actually." Aerin's look was

challenging. "You know I've always struggled with my weight."

Olivia shifted uncomfortably. She hadn't intended to bring up any sore topics, just to tell Aerin how good she looked. Thinking back on it, probably not a great idea to do that, either. She backpedaled quickly. "I just mean objectively, your face has better blood flow than it did before, sort of like if you were pregnant. Oh. I guess I should ask, since it could affect the test results. Are you pregnant?"

"I'm not pregnant."

"Okay, that's good. I mean, unless you want to be pregnant. In which case, I wish you the best. Anyway, where were we? Right, the EEG helmet I want to give you is right here." She held up the shiny black helmet that would take readings for a twenty-four-hour period and then transmit them wirelessly to a program on her computer. She pushed her fingers against the thick plastic cover, trying in vain to jab them through. Anything to distract her from the way she fell all over her words. When she finally raised her eyes to look at Aerin, she found a hint of a smile on her face.

"Can you wear this for twenty-four hours starting tomorrow? I don't want it off campus for too long."

"Wait, I have to wear it all day? Tomorrow? No, I have clients." Aerin looked mortified at the thought of wearing a very uncool helmet around all day. Olivia didn't blame her. She wouldn't be caught dead in public in that thing.

"Okay, the next day?"

"Um, no. But I will find time. I just can't promise it will be before the weekend."

Olivia shrugged. "Okay. Let me fit this to your head."

She felt unmistakable heat coming off Aerin as she stood above her and put the helmet on. After a few adjustments, it fit snugly and was sending real-time data to Olivia's laptop.

"Shit," she muttered.

"What?"

"Nothing, just similar to what we saw before. Crazy amounts of activity." Olivia stared at the reading on the screen and struggled to make sense of it. "Can you do me a favor and take a deep breath? Think of something that makes you calm."

She waited for a moment and saw no perceptible change in the EEG.

"Did you do it?"

"Yeah. I was thinking about being in the woods." Aerin gave her a knowing look and Olivia felt the heat rise to her cheeks.

"Okay, well, wear this for a day and a night. I promise it's not terrible to sleep in. I want to see what happens when you fall asleep."

Aerin blushed and Olivia sucked in a breath as she realized what she'd said. This whole conversation had somehow gone off the rails. She certainly hadn't meant to follow Aerin's suggestive answer with an innuendo.

The first time they'd had sex was in a tent in the woods at Jesus camp. Afterward, every time they'd slept together, Aerin had fallen asleep first and Olivia had watched her breathe, her face innocent and beautiful. It all stood out like oddly distant memories from somebody else in some other life.

"So, I'll—"

"You should—"

Olivia cleared her throat. "Take your time with this, just be careful. It's a little fragile and it has its issues, but it should give us what we want."

"Don't worry. That's why I'm in the business I'm in." Aerin stood, pointedly looking into Olivia's eyes. "Because we're all a little fragile and we all have our issues. I'll take good care of this and give you a call when I'm ready to give it back."

Olivia felt the words deep in her chest, even as she wanted to roll her eyes at how corny they were. She watched Aerin cradle the helmet under her arm as she turned the corner, leaving nothing but a faint scent of burnt sugar to ghost the room.

CHAPTER TWELVE

It was a blustery winter day in Chicago. The wind whipped through Olivia's fleece hat as she shivered her way to Lincoln Park. Daria had texted her an hour ago with instructions to meet her there, and she'd only just finished her work in the lab. She was not exactly in a hurry.

Sorry, on my way, she wrote as she stepped off the El. They'd spent a lot of time in the conservatory over the summer and Olivia had been happy to make the walk then, wandering through the wide green streets of the city. In January, though, she silently resented Daria for asking her to make the trip.

Are you walking? Daria texted.

Yup.

Take a cab, babe, I've been waiting here forever. I have a surprise.

Olivia stopped and reread the message. Take a cab? Neither of them ever spent money they didn't have on superfluous things like cabs. It could only mean one thing. Daria had planned something for her, and there were only a few things Daria would have planned. Thank God she'd disabled the "read" notification on her phone. She pulled up a streaming video app that would eat the battery. If Daria asked why she didn't take a cab, she'd just pretend her phone died before she saw the message. Shitty, yes. Necessary? Probably.

Olivia picked up her pace to stave off the cold, blowing a hard breath between her mittened hands that left tiny icicles on the fabric. She spotted a coffee shop across the street and went inside. The barista was cute and queer, about her age, and she smiled as they handed her the steaming latte. They touched Olivia's hand as she took it, igniting a trickle of pleasure that left her giddy. It occurred to her that she'd never felt giddy with Daria. Maybe in the beginning, but their relationship had soured, the spark buried under too many layers of ash and ennui.

Maybe Daria had planned some anniversary thing. It had been, what, a year and two months? Hardly anything worth noting. With Daria, though, you never knew. She would celebrate the first day of December, then forget to plan for Christmas. Not that it bothered Olivia, who was done with anything resembling a Christian holiday. Only one thing happened on Christmas, her yearly perfunctory phone call with her mom.

She continued down the street. Took a left, a right, and then the park was in front of her, no hint of the summer grass under the thick coating of snow glazed with ice. The surface shimmered so brightly that Olivia couldn't look at it directly. A few people wandered around the zoo, hunkered so far into layers of warm clothing that you could only see their winter weary eyes. The entire city had already been done in by the eternal cold and it was only January.

The conservatory loomed to her left and she reluctantly wandered toward it. Daria could be so intense sometimes, overflowing with childish excitement. Olivia often found herself playing the adult, and she hated herself for it. The decent sex kept her around. That and the ability to share the rent with someone. Daria was the first person she'd allowed to love her since Aerin. The devotion had at first felt safe but had dissolved into irritation over the months.

"Olivia, what in the world took you so long?" Daria leaned out the conservatory door and motioned her inside with sorely underdressed arms. Her usually severe eye makeup was a little toned down today, which frightened Olivia. Daria had actually made an effort, tried to look like someone who possessed taste.

She shook the thought from her head, angry at Daria for her own cruelty. Inside the glass building stood four of their mutual friends, three of them a bit wary. Daria looked at her hopefully, kneading her hands and lifting on the balls of her feet. She wore a denim jacket and black slacks. Her mahogany hair curled around her shoulders. She looked good, attractive. If they'd been at home, Olivia would have straddled Daria and fucked her right there on the couch. In public, though, Daria made her uncomfortable. Olivia knew it was the shame of being seen with someone so gauche, but would never say so.

"Olivia, I brought you here to ask you something," she said.

Olivia pleaded with her eyes. Don't make a fool of yourself, Daria. Read the room.

Daria stepped closer and took Olivia's hands. She began to ask the Question as Olivia shook her head. It seemed to happen in slow motion. It took Daria a second to understand Olivia's refusal, at which point her face journeyed through the stages of proposal failure. Confusion, denial, realization, embarrassment. Olivia cringed as their hands separated, feeling the entire room, plant and human, watching her, waiting.

"Why?" Daria's voice was soft, almost imperceptible as it bounced off the glass dome and dropped at her feet.

Olivia couldn't get into this here, not now, not ever if

she could help it. Couldn't they just go on as they had? A reasonable level of commitment and monogamy, but nothing more. No finality, a possibility that their relationship might not be her last. That there could be something better for Olivia. That there already had been.

"Daria, can we talk about this at home?" Olivia said in a hushed voice. Their friends had begun to look intently at some of the flowers near the door.

"Is it me, or is it you?" Daria's words were biting, her gaze penetrating.

No, thought Olivia, neither. She shook her head, jiggling the pieces of her memory back in place. Even after all these years, all the heartache, Aerin had stayed with her, loving Olivia the way nobody else could. "It's not you. I should go. I'll stay with some friends from school tonight and we can talk in the morning."

She turned to leave. A heartbreaking silence followed her out the door, but when she stepped into the heaviness of winter, the sky was a little brighter.

CHAPTER THIRTEEN

Aerin and Zoe stepped into the dimly lit belly of Indianapolis's most famous jazz club. Zoe immediately spotted Ben at the bar and ran to him. Great, Aerin thought, ditched the moment they got there for the boyfriend. The preshow music pulsed through her, her body throbbing with every bass note. It felt heavy, like pain bordering on pleasure, and she stayed in the entrance, weighing whether she wanted to be there at all.

"Hey, you coming over?" Zoe shouted. She trotted back over to where Aerin stood rooted to the floor.

"Um, don't you think the music's kind of loud?" Aerin struggled to concentrate on Zoe's presence as the dominating sound wove through her. Ever since the lake incident, noises seemed amplified, and she'd begun to avoid loud places as much as possible. The club's music wasn't as awful as the noise that arose from within her own head sometimes, but it did, in the same way, drill into her like steel bolts. She couldn't remember why she'd agreed to come out tonight, other than to get her mind off, well, her mind.

"Loud? Not really, but if you want, I can ask them to turn it down. The band will be playing soon anyway and that'll be better for all of us. I hate this weird techno-jazz crap."

Aerin took a deep breath and willed herself to relegate the music to the back of her mind. Unsurprisingly, it worked, the same way she'd been controlling her emotions and body lately with just a single thought. "I'm okay. How about a drink?"

"You read my mind. Let's go."

At the bar, Aerin took a seat between Zoe and one of Ben's bandmates, a postdoc at the university.

"Stanton Carlile Jones," he said, gently taking her outstretched hand. "The third." The soft bar lighting reflected off his bald head.

Aerin was immediately charmed. "Aerin McLeary, the first."

Stanton smiled and released her hand, a faraway look in his eyes. He blinked rapidly for a moment. "Always a pleasure to meet friends of friends. What is it you do for work?" Stanton asked.

"I'm a therapist. I'm trying to be, at least. It's not going so well." Aerin took her drink from the bartender and glanced back at Stanton, whose focus was now solely on her. She felt seen for the first time in a while.

"What's got you down?" he asked.

Aerin shrugged, unsure if she should be telling strangers about the telepathy. "I just had a tough case, that's all. And, well, I'm the only therapist in Tireville, you know, tiny town about an hour from here, who isn't somehow affiliated with a church. It's not a lucrative market."

Stanton smiled widely. "Well, it sounds like you're exactly where you're supposed to be, doing what you're supposed to be doing."

He disconcertingly looked through her again and blinked, but she believed him without hesitation. "Thank you," she said. Stanton's eyes glimmered.

On the other side of her, she heard a stool squeak across the floor and Ben came around to tap Stanton on the shoulder.

"Hey, man, it's a few minutes till showtime. Aerin, I see you've met my good friend Stanton. Best saxophone player in the flyover states and computer science researcher extraordinaire."

"You're too much." Stanton clapped Ben on the shoulder. "Ben's got a pair of chops on him that I haven't seen in ages. In fact, I wouldn't trust anyone else to play my songs."

"You write the music yourselves?" Aerin looked at them both, impressed. She hadn't heard it yet, but from what Zoe said, she assumed it was at least decent.

"Stanton writes most of them, but I have a special one for Zoe. Speaking of which, we should probably go and get ready," Ben said.

Stanton nodded. "Well, Miss McLeary, sorry to leave you so soon, but it looks like our time is over, for now. Nice to meet you." Stanton smiled brilliantly and stood. Something about him held Aerin's gaze until he disappeared from view. Ben followed soon after.

Zoe, who had been occupied talking to a third bandmate, slid her drink closer to Aerin's. "Whoa there. Got the hots for Stanton much? Geez, you're practically glowing with lust."

Aerin snapped out of her thoughts and looked at Zoe, suddenly remembering herself. "Oh. Yeah. I mean, no, not in that way. Just, something about him, don't you think?" Aerin dove for words that described what she meant, but she couldn't find them. Stanton's magnetism wasn't sexual but was unexpected in its ease. If she hadn't been sure she'd just met him for the first time, she'd have thought they shared a years-long deep connection.

"Hey, look who it is," Zoe said urgently, nudging Aerin with her elbow.

Aerin didn't have to turn around to see who had walked in. She felt the syrupy sweetness of long-lost love and the electric possibility of new friendship from across the room.

"Olivia," she whispered. She could feel the moment of recognition as Olivia looked at the bar. First Stanton and now this. Her brain spun and she suddenly felt hungry even after her highly caloric dinner.

"Who's the hot older lady that she's with? Are they together? Damn, is all I have to say. She would not have to be the last woman on Earth for me to—"

"Jody." Aerin stared at her drink.

Zoe stared at her. "Wait, did you know they were coming tonight?" Aerin shook her head. "How did you know it was them? Did you suddenly develop a sixth sense or something?"

Aerin turned and stared into Zoe's eyes. She saw them widen in shock.

"Oh, okay. So, the Incident made you into some kind of superhero mutant. What, like Lake Woman or something?"

Aerin grasped her arm and squeezed. "Zoe, be quiet," she said in a rough whisper. She glanced around them. "I don't want anyone to know what I can see without seeing. I don't even understand it myself."

Zoe blinked in disbelief. "What am I thinking right now?"

"I can't just—"

"Aerin. Look at me. What am I thinking right now?" Zoe propped her elbow on the bar and waited for Aerin's assessment.

After a long stare at Zoe, Aerin felt the thoughts creeping through. And they contained images she didn't want to see. "Really, Zoe?"

"What?"

"You're thinking about having sex with Jody. To be more specific, you're thinking about how hot it would be for her to go down on you. She's not that attractive." Aerin raised an eyebrow as Zoe turned bright red.

"Oh. Well, that was like way back there, I guess. I was thinking of a potato for you, though. You were supposed to say 'potato.'" She shifted uncomfortably on her barstool. "Sorry."

Aerin tried to suppress a smile but failed miserably. "It was pretty hot. I didn't know you were into that."

Zoe bit her lower lip and squeezed Aerin's shoulder. "I didn't either. And Jesus, stop getting off on my mind porn. Speaking of which, they're headed over."

"I know," Aerin said.

"Right."

She didn't turn around until Olivia was directly behind her, and when she did, her pulse began to race. Olivia was wearing a sexy gray suit that hugged her slight frame, its jacket casually open to a cerulean T-shirt that made her think of a soft summer breeze. Aerin swallowed hard and watched Olivia's pupils dilate in return.

"Hi," Olivia said in a voice that came out huskier than intended. She blushed.

"Hi. Drink?"

Olivia blinked as if suddenly realizing she was somewhere entirely different from where she expected to be. "Uh, no. No, I'm okay. Hey, nice to see you again. We'll be in touch about the, about the EEG. It looks like the band's coming out, so I'm going to get a spot." She turned quickly and disappeared into the crowd.

"I saw that." Zoe slid closer and put her arm around Aerin's shoulders. "She is so into you, just like the old days."

Aerin chuckled. "She's not. Plus, you were weren't even around in the old days."

"I have a very active imagination. Also, she is." Zoe took a swig of her drink and cringed at the alcohol burn.

"Zoe, I basically broke up her family and then married the first guy who showed interest in me, so I think she's not actually interested in dating me. Again." A sick feeling crept into Aerin's stomach, a combination of hunger mixed with alcohol and a huge dose of guilt. She threw back the rest of her old-fashioned and stood. "Let's get out there. They're about to go on."

The music that filled the room was like nothing Aerin had ever heard, a funky jazz sound that made her spine tingle and her body move to the rhythm. She closed her eyes and listened, the busy part of her brain occupied by the music and allowing her to relax for the first time in weeks. She was lost in the jazz when she felt someone come up behind her and press their body against hers. She figured it must be Zoe, so she smiled and kept dancing. When she opened her eyes a few moments later, she spotted Zoe at the foot of the stage, gazing longingly at Ben, who was really milking her attention on the baritone sax. Alarmed, she turned to see an older drunk man behind her.

He smiled lecherously and Aerin grimaced. She moved through the crowd nearer to Zoe, shaking at the thought of the stranger's body on hers. She wanted to believe that he'd stayed where she left him, but she could hear him following, looking for her amongst the moving bodies. She changed tactics and turned away from the stage, pushing out of the crowd, feeling his slimy presence behind her the whole time. As she headed for the bar, where surely the bartender would help her lose this creep, she felt an arm snake around her waist and draw her in. She almost screamed at the touch, until she realized who the arm belonged to.

"Hey, I've got you. Play along," Olivia whispered in her ear. "There you are, babe. I was looking all over for you," she said, loud enough so the man, who had stopped in his tracks, could hear. "I had to step out for a call, from the guys down at the police station, where I work."

Aerin tried not to laugh as she watched the man shrink into himself, then flee into the far corner. "Thank you." The hand remained on her hip, but Olivia didn't seem to notice. "You know, I think I'm done with tonight already. Let me see if Zoe can take me home." Aerin hated to leave halfway through, but between the way the preshow music made her feel and now this, she just wanted to crawl into bed.

Olivia nodded and quickly took her hand from Aerin, stuffing it in her pocket. Aerin made a beeline for the stage, Olivia at her back the whole time. She was comforted by Olivia's willingness to pretend they were together. Aerin couldn't help but wish she hadn't screwed everything up the first time. Maybe they'd be married by now. Maybe she'd have the kids she'd always dreamed about, a career that paid the bills and then some, and a little house in the suburbs, or maybe even a condo in the city. She could imagine it clearly, and a wave of regret passed through her. Zoe was leaning on the stage and bobbing her head in time to the music when Aerin tapped her on the shoulder.

"Hey, where have you been?" Zoe asked.

Aerin put her mouth close to Zoe's ear. "Around. Listen, I'm not feeling well. Any chance we could leave really soon?"

Zoe turned around with a pathetic pout on her face. "Okay, I guess, if we have to. I wanted to stay longer, though, because Ben said he has a piece he wrote for me."

"Oh," Aerin said, trying to figure out if there were any other options. Now that she'd had time to think about the horrible violation she'd felt from the drunk guy, she couldn't wait go home and take a really hot shower.

Olivia leaned over and spoke into Aerin's ear. "What about your husband? Can't he come pick you up?"

Aerin shook her head and Zoe's eyebrows shot up. She sighed and held her left hand in front of Olivia's face. She pointed at her bare ring finger and Olivia mouthed, "Oh." She could hear the confusion in Zoe and Olivia's minds, and added to the music coming from an amp in front of them, it was all too much. She pushed back through the crowd, through the door, and into the cool night, drinking the air like a balm. The quiet pillowed her ears and the moon shined brightly, reflecting off car windshields at the dealership across the street.

She heard the heavy door open and shut behind her, felt Olivia slowly moving closer.

"Why didn't you tell me?"

Aerin shrugged. "I don't know. There didn't seem like a good time to bring it up."

Olivia scuffed the ground with her leather shoe. "So, you wanted me to believe you were still married to the asshole you started dating immediately after you moved on from our relationship, which apparently wasn't too important to you, given that you never got in touch with me, ever."

Aerin gave a half laugh. "Jesus. That does make me sound horrible, but you know it wasn't that simple."

"Yeah, no kidding. Look, you don't owe me anything. Not anymore. I would have appreciated a heads up, though. Especially since I brought it up a couple of times now and you basically let me believe that you were still with that scumbag."

Aerin didn't correct her. If she'd been in Olivia's place, she'd have hated him, too. "I'm sorry." She looked at Olivia, who stared intently at the ground. The pain illuminated deeply etched worry lines and it was clear she'd never let the heartbreak go in all the years since they'd parted ways. But then, neither had she.

She took Olivia's hand and squeezed before letting it drop. "If being around me brings up too many negative feelings for you, I get it. We don't have to be friends and you don't have to help me with my brain stuff. I don't want you to feel obligated in any way."

Olivia nodded and finally looked at Aerin. Okay, so she agreed. They were officially done as new acquaintances. Aerin breathed a sigh of relief that she would no longer be constantly confronted with her past mistakes, but the regret remained. It might diminish over time, but it would never go away. Nobody got a do-over, that's what she told her clients. They had to live in the present, not dwell in the past. She'd do well to take her own advice.

"I'm going to call a cab, I think. Zoe's going to want to wait until her song comes on and I'm exhausted." Aerin took out her phone and brought up a ridesharing app.

"Wait." Olivia rocked back and forth on her feet. "I'll give you a ride. I should pick up the EEG anyway. You did wear it, right?"

"Yeah, I wore it for about eighteen hours straight," she said distractedly, still putting her location into the app. "Olivia, you don't have to drive me home. It's ridiculously far out of your way."

"It is, I know." Olivia looked at the sky, searching for what she wanted to say. "It just seems like we have a lot to catch up on."

Aerin was dumbfounded. Did this mean Olivia wasn't getting rid of her just yet? Unexpected, but she wouldn't pass up a ride if it gave her another chance to show Olivia she'd changed. "Okay. If you're sure."

Olivia didn't look sure, but she nodded anyway. "Do you need to tell Zoe first?"

"Right," Aerin said taking out her phone to send a text. She'd forgotten about Zoe for a minute. "All set."

Olivia led her to a blue sports car and hit the unlock

button. As the taillights flashed, Aerin chuckled. "Now why doesn't it surprise me that you have a fast car?"

She could see Olivia's face light up as she slid into her leather seat. "I love it. So do the cops. They make a lot of money off me. So, strap yourself in."

"Okay, but don't go too fast. Precious scientific cargo right here."

CHAPTER FOURTEEN

It was two in the afternoon, three days after Olivia and Aerin were caught in the church pew by Olivia's father. Three days into her new, hellish life. Olivia cried the entire time she packed her bags for Chicago. It wasn't clear where the tears could possibly be coming from anymore, but they continued to flow from some bottomless source. She heard a noise in the doorway, her mother softly clearing her throat. Olivia wiped her nose.

"Can I come in?"

"I guess," Olivia said in a strained voice that didn't seem her own.

Her mother sat on the bed next to the half-filled suitcase Olivia would be taking with her tonight. Her bus left at 8:15 and would roll into downtown Chicago three hours later. Her grandparents would be there to pick her up. These were things she knew would happen, but she couldn't reconcile them with her life. This happened to other people. Other people got kicked out of their houses for being gay. Not her. Not brilliant, loving Olivia, who'd lived in Tireville her entire life and had friends, close ones, maybe even some who would still be friendly even if they knew she liked girls.

Olivia sank to her knees in front of her suitcase and rested her forehead on the edge of the bed. She inhaled deeply. This room smelled like Aerin, like summer and freshly cut grass, like love that was supposed to last forever. She started crying again and her mother rested a hand on her shoulder. It was meant to be comforting, but it felt alien. After all, she'd only just realized the capacity of her mother to impart the cruelness she associated with her father. He wasn't the only one kicking her out.

"You know I'm sorry we have to do this, but it will be for the best, sweetie," her mother said. "Your grandparents are much more cosmopolitan than we are out here. They'll understand better."

Olivia wanted to shout, to rebel. She wanted to inflict upon her mother a wound just a fraction of the size of her own, but they'd worn her down. They'd convinced her so thoroughly that she wanted to go live with her grandparents that it almost seemed like her own idea. Maybe it would be better to start over. At least she wouldn't have to see Aerin again.

She was angry, hurt, and confused. She'd expected some kind of apology from Aerin for running away but hadn't heard from her at all, not even through one of their usual locker notes. She wondered if Aerin knew that in a few hours, she'd be gone for good. A part of her hoped Aerin would wake up tomorrow morning and realize the huge mistake she'd made. She wanted Aerin to try and fail to find her in Chicago. At least then they'd both be hurting.

"You promise you'll bring Mr. Piddles up next weekend?" Olivia asked.

Her father had tried to get rid of the bird, but in a weak show of solidarity with her only child, her mother fought him. "It's all she has, Martin," her mother had said, and he'd relented.

"Yes, I promise. I'll be up on Saturday with everything else." Her mother sighed. "Do you want me to help you pack?"

Olivia didn't want her touching anything, but it seemed easier to agree.

A few hours later, she sat on the bed next to her mother, holding her hand.

A shadow passed by the doorway and he appeared. "It's time," he said.

Chapter Fifteen

Olivia slid the car into fifth gear, her hand lingering on the sleek shift, glowing from Aerin's appreciation of her WRX, her baby. She tried not to think about how good it made her feel to drive a beautiful, sexy woman home, because that woman was capable of ruining Olivia's life again. She tore her eyes from the road for a moment to glance at Aerin.

"So, tell me about you and Josh." She hadn't said his name in years, and it hurt a little less than she'd expected to finally utter it aloud.

She felt Aerin look at her for a long moment. "We got divorced," she finally said.

"Oh. I figured he died. You know, marriage being forever and everything. Why'd you get divorced?"

Aerin didn't speak for a while and Olivia congratulated herself on the jab. She watched the occasional farmhouse go by, windows so warmly lit that she wanted to stop in and be welcomed by a big hug and a pie. Just like the old days, when her father would take her along to make house calls. Sometimes a good memory of her childhood crept in when she was least expecting it.

Aerin's voice drew her from her thoughts. "I started dating Josh right after you because I was scared. I married him because I was scared and I finally divorced him because I was sick of living in constant fear," Aerin said.

Olivia didn't respond.

"Your dad, he told me the way I could repent was to get married and have kids. And I was an idiot back then, so I listened to him."

Olivia let out a breath. She already felt closer to Aerin, united in their hatred of her father. "He's dead to me," she said.

"He's not a good person. Anyway, I married Josh and he wanted kids, but for some reason I just couldn't picture myself having his baby. I actually took birth control and just never told him." She laughed a little.

Olivia cringed at the thought of Aerin having unprotected sex with Josh. "So, did he finally figure that out and leave you?"

"No, I left him. I'm not proud of it, but I cheated on him and it made me realize that I wasn't who I wanted to be."

Olivia almost slammed on the brakes. Perfect Aerin, the perfect Baptist and perfect hometown girl, broke all the rules and had an affair? This had to be some alternate reality. She blew out a long breath. "Wow. Where'd you meet him?"

"Her," Aerin said simply.

Olivia's heart skipped a beat and plummeted into her stomach like a lead ball.

"Yeah, I had an affair with a woman. I've never said this to anyone except Zoe, but I'm pretty sure I'm not a hundred percent straight. Far from it, actually."

Olivia ground her teeth and gripped the wheel. She didn't know whether to feel angry that she'd been dumped for a failed heterosexual experiment or thrilled that Aerin finally realized what Olivia had suspected, wanted, for years.

"Say something," Aerin said.

Olivia swallowed hard. "I don't know what to say, honestly."

"Can you give me a hint about what you're thinking? I'm trying not to read your mind, but it's really hard to block it out, so at some point, it's just going to come through."

Her admission tipped Olivia into anger. She couldn't even process all of this privately. "Well, why don't you read my mind and then tell me how the hell I'm supposed to feel. You were everything to me, Aerin. Everything. Then, after what happened, it was like I was invisible. To you and everyone else in Tireville. You never even called or tried to find me. Now you come back into my life and it was all a lie?" She shook her head. "I'm so glad it only took you half a lifetime to figure out who you are. How the fuck do you want me to feel, happy for you?" Olivia said, surprised to find tears rolling down her face. She couldn't remember the last time she'd cried, and in the car driving eighty miles per hour down the highway was certainly not an ideal place for it.

Aerin spoke quietly, as if she'd expected this response. "You left me, too. I never got to say good-bye. I never even got a chance to make it up to you. You were in Chicago, which I know wasn't your choice, but I had no way to get in touch. Your parents wouldn't give me your new number."

Olivia sniffled. "You asked them for it?"

"Of course. I was heartbroken. I'm sorry for the way things happened and I wish I could go back and do everything over, but I can't. Things have changed. I've changed. I just hope you give me a chance to show you that. As a friend, I mean. I want to be your friend again."

Aerin's words bounced off Olivia like rubber. Even though she'd had the decency to try and get in touch with her at the time, Aerin ended up marrying someone she didn't love.

Because it seemed easier than finding her and apologizing? Olivia felt exhausted, emotionally drained, her thoughts not even making sense to herself anymore. She wished she hadn't given Aerin this ride after all.

"We're almost there," Aerin said. Olivia looked at her and she shrugged. "Sorry, I can't help it. Your thoughts come in loud and clear when there's no other noise."

"Wonderful." Olivia turned the radio to a rock station and put the volume up louder than usual.

They drove the rest of the way without talking, Olivia stepping on the gas a little harder than she usually did to shorten the ride. She thought of everything she could besides her own feelings. The article she was writing on neurocognitive elasticity, Mr. Piddles, baseball. Finally they pulled into Aerin's driveway.

"Do you want me to get you the machine?"

Olivia snapped out of her exhausted haze. "Huh?"

"The EEG. Do you want it? Are you okay to drive? You seem pretty tired."

Olivia suppressed a yawn and nodded. "I'm fine. I'll come in and get it." So I won't have to see you again anytime soon, she thought.

She followed Aerin into the house, filled with vibrant patterns and colors. A painting of a forest scene hung next to some prayer flags. A purple tapestry draped a beige armchair. The house screamed Aerin through and through, fascinating and bold, the Aerin she'd known all those years ago. The off-white couch looked especially inviting and she was eyeing it pretty hard when Aerin invited her to have a seat. Moments later, Olivia leaned onto the large, comfortable pillow in the corner and shut her eyes. Just for a moment. Just so she could drive home.

Chapter Sixteen

Olivia blinked at the unfamiliar living room, light streaming in from the windows on either side, casting the pale blue walls in a stunning tropical hue. It took her a moment to remember where she could possibly be.

"Hey, you're up, finally." Aerin smiled brilliantly as she brought over a mug of hot coffee. Coffee that Olivia desperately needed to figure out how the hell she'd ended up having a sleepover at Aerin's.

"I'm sorry. I have no idea why I couldn't drive home." Olivia coughed, her throat completely dry, and took a sip of the coffee.

"It's fine, really." Aerin nudged Olivia's legs over so she could sit on the couch.

Olivia shook her head. She hadn't spent a night out of her own house since she'd bought it four years ago. She liked to wake up in a familiar bed molded to her body, with all her earthly possessions just a short walk away. Her life was more straightforward that way. "It's just weird, that's all. Totally out of character for me." She sat up and sipped her drink. Pieces of last night's conversation flashed in her mind and she realized she wasn't angry anymore. In fact, she was curious about this new Aerin and the woman who'd finally helped her come out of her shell. "So, tell me about her."

Aerin put her mug down and crossed her legs, deliberately, it seemed to Olivia. "Who?"

"Aerin, don't do this with me. I know you can read my mind and I know you know who I'm talking about. Look, if we're going to try to be friends or whatever, you have to cut the bullshit."

Aerin crossed her arms and sighed. "Okay, fine. I was just trying to pretend to be normal." She looked at the ceiling for a moment, the perfect angle for Olivia to gaze at the skin on her neck that she'd kissed so many times, intimate and completely foreign at the same time.

"She was a nurse at the hospital where I used to work. Her name was Shonda and she was also married, but her husband let her sleep with women."

Interesting arrangement. "So, what happened?" Olivia asked.

"Well, she was gorgeous, still is, I assume, and she saw the looks I was giving her one day. So, after work, we went and parked her car somewhere." Aerin blushed and sipped her coffee.

"You made out in her car like teenagers?"

Aerin shrugged.

"Oh my God, you had sex with her in the back seat of a car? In public? Perfect little Aerin sneaking around behind her husband's back. I'm honestly shocked." Olivia chuckled bitterly.

"You're making it sound like some kind of salacious thing, but really it was sweet. It only lasted a couple of really satisfying weeks before she got tired of me," Aerin said.

Olivia huffed. "Tired of you?" Her body buzzed as she recalled how much she would have sacrificed to have a little more of Aerin, even one more hug. How could anyone get tired of her?

"Anyway, that's the whole story. It's not that exciting."

Olivia slowly nodded. "Thanks for telling me. I'm sorry I got defensive last night." Her mind raced. She was not nearly as over Aerin as she'd thought. Aerin held her gaze for a moment, unabashedly reading Olivia's mind. Olivia could feel the intrusion as a subtle, swirling magnetism behind her forehead.

Aerin cleared her throat and stood. "I'm getting more coffee. Do you want another cup?"

A sudden craving for more coffee took over Olivia's thoughts, then quickly vanished. "You know, I should get going. I have to feed Mr. Piddles. Can you get the EEG helmet for me? I'll take a look at the results when I get home."

Aerin brought it to her, reluctantly, it seemed.

"Thanks for letting me crash here. I guess I'll see you soon," Olivia said.

Aerin remained expressionless. "Yeah, see you soon." She held the front door open.

Olivia shivered at the cool morning air and drew her wrinkled suit jacket in, taking one last look at Aerin, who watched her from the doorway. A burst of heat passed through her as she realized what it looked like, leaving Aerin's house early in the morning. She blushed and slid into her familiar leather front seat, eager to return to the safety of her insulated life.

CHAPTER SEVENTEEN

Olivia was four when her parents moved from Illinois to Indiana for Martin Ando's appointment at the Tireville Baptist Church. The first time she visited the church, she clung to her mother's side, staring in awe at the giant silver cross dominating the front of the room. They were the first ones in the building that Sunday morning and Olivia's footsteps echoed against the cavernous ceiling. The whiteness of the walls added to her childish notion that this church must be a portal to heaven, in all its brightness and enormity. And if it could reach heaven, then maybe she was an angel sent to help her father bring people closer to God.

"Olivia, you have to be good today," he had said that morning as he pulled a purple jumper over her head. "You have to help Daddy show the people how much God loves them, okay? You're daddy's little angel."

Olivia nodded and adjusted her tights. She had to pee and her father always hated it when she didn't say something before she got all dressed up. She would have to hold it until they got to church, when he would be in his office pacing and the familiar fear of displeasing him would lift.

She was an angel, a bringer of peace, a small hope in a world that had fallen into sin, her father said almost nightly as he practiced his preaching. But an angel sent from heaven wouldn't have peed down her leg as she walked toward the pulpit, so Olivia pretended her body belonged to someone else, a sinner, and she watched it from her position above the pews, flying, pure as her father wanted her to be.

"Olivia, did you wet your pants?" her mother asked. She hated making her parents angry, but at least her mother wouldn't slap her across the face. She shook her head, soaring above the congregants trickling in from the lobby.

"I didn't," she said.

"Let's get you out of these tights so your father doesn't see." Her mother dragged her back toward the small crowd of gray-haired ladies chatting over coffee in one group, their husbands in another. Her wrist ached as her mother pulled her down a small flight of stairs into the bathroom. In the biggest stall, Olivia stood stiffly as her tights and underwear were yanked from her small body. She had stopped flying and the fluorescent lights of the church bathroom stung her eyes with their harsh brightness.

"I have an extra pair of panties, at least." Her mother sighed disappointedly. Olivia put them on and they went back upstairs. On the way up, she saw her mother drop the soiled tights into the garbage.

Later, her father would yell at her for losing her tights, asking her how she'd be able to contribute the money to buy more. Olivia didn't understand money back then, but she understood anger and she vowed to do whatever she could to make sure she wasn't the cause.

CHAPTER EIGHTEEN

The Mobil gas station just outside of Tireville seemed like a safe place to stop and fill the car, empty from the drive last night. Olivia heard her stomach groan as she pulled up to the pump. Not many people were out this early on a Saturday. After she pumped the gas, she left her car in its spot and went inside. She glanced quickly at the attendant to make sure she didn't know him, then made her way to the small selection of snacks.

She was reading the ingredients on the back of a granola bar when the door jingled and someone stepped up to the counter.

"Do you have Pop-Tarts?" a boy asked. His voice cracked as he thanked the attendant for what Olivia assumed was a nod in the right direction.

The boy's footsteps came closer and she instinctively stiffened. She didn't have the presence of mind to deal with people this morning. The kid appeared next to her and grabbed a pack of strawberry Pop-Tarts off the shelf next to her.

"Is that your car out there?" he asked.

Olivia glanced over at him, taken aback by his directness. "Huh?"

"The blue WRX. Is it yours?"

"Why?" She looked over his short dark hair and basketball shorts. Something about his golden brown eyes and arched eyebrows looked familiar. Good, she thought, Tireville could use a few more non-Caucasian people. He looked like a nice kid. "Yeah, it's mine."

"Cool. I definitely want a car like that when I get my license."

"Oh yeah? It's pretty fast. You have to be a good driver to handle it," Olivia said, smirking at his eagerness.

He nodded vigorously. "I practice on my video games. I'll be really good by then."

"Well, good luck. I hope you get your car."

The door jingled again as someone walked in. "Emmanuel? Are you still in here?"

Olivia froze. The voice sounded unmistakable, though she hadn't heard its pure form in years. She held her breath as a once-familiar face emerged from around the corner of the aisle. Before she could form words, Emmanuel piped up.

"Hey, Mom, she's the one with the cool car." He looked back and forth at the two of them, confused. Olivia stared at her mother with a clenched jaw. Neither spoke for a long moment.

"Olivia." Mariko sounded resigned, as if she'd expected this moment to happen someday. "It's good to see you." Mariko's face sagged and Olivia knew she was lying, but they couldn't very well unsee each other, as much as they both wanted to.

"Wait. This is my sister? That car is basically in my family?" Emmanuel beamed and looked at Olivia in a new, respectful way.

Mariko glared at him. "Emmanuel, go wait in the car."

"But my Pop-Tarts!"

"Now," Mariko said. He hung his head and moped out of

the store, shooting Olivia one final, longing look before the door slammed behind him.

"You look well," Mariko said shortly.

Olivia could see her mother's emotions swimming beneath the surface. She knew that if her mother set them free, it would be tantamount to admitting she'd made a mistake by sending Olivia away.

"I'm doing fine. I'm going to pay for this and go. Nice seeing you." Olivia pushed past Mariko, who stood rooted to the spot with her arms crossed.

"Olivia." Time seemed to stop and Olivia's throat went dry. Her heart skipped a beat, an automatic reaction from childhood that time had not erased. "I'm sorry for what your father did."

Olivia stopped mid-step and twirled around, her eyes penetrating her mother's. No. She did not get to apologize. She'd have to bear the burden of betrayal as Olivia bore its scars.

"He wasn't my only parent," she said in a low voice. Her mother let out a shaky breath as Olivia turned away. At the register, she put the snack down. "I don't want this anymore." The attendant shrugged.

Outside, she slid into her car and started the engine. As she pulled forward, she saw Emmanuel's face pressed to the inside of Mariko's white Ford Explorer. She gave him a little wave and he smiled. He seemed like a cool little guy. Hopefully Mariko and Martin Ando wouldn't fuck up their second chance at raising a child.

CHAPTER NINETEEN

Olivia pulled a hefty stack of fresh pages from the printer tray. She'd printed out an hour's worth of EEG data in order to show Jody the seriousness of Aerin's readings. The pages were densely colored in drying ink and Jody's eyes widened as she spread them out on her desk. The clustered peaks and valleys of Aerin's EEG showed heavy brain activity indicative of a seizure pattern, and it went on for the entirety of her record.

Olivia glanced from the pages to Jody's face. "So, my machine at home was correct."

Jody huffed. "This is crazy, right? Nobody's brain should be doing this."

Olivia agreed. "Not for this long. It's been weeks since the first reading. This is completely unsustainable. It's like she's unlocked a whole level in her brain so the neurons are firing twice as fast and twice as many are in use at once. No wonder she's losing weight." Olivia stared at her hands, deep in thought. "She had some kind of trauma to her brain in the lake, and whatever it was, it caused her to basically level up in life. Jesus, if I can figure out what it was and then replicate it, well, this would be huge for the future of humanity. And of course my career."

Jody leaned back in her chair and smiled. "Interesting. Part of me thought you'd get too emotionally involved to see the potential in the science. By the way, thanks again for leaving me at the club the other night."

Olivia grimaced. She'd remembered to call Jody as soon as she got home the next morning, hours too late. "I'm so, so, so sorry, for the millionth time. I honestly have no idea how it happened."

"I know, I know. You were in a trance or something. I'm just teasing. I personally think you were drunk. Drunk on lust for your ex-lover."

"Don't say 'lover' ever again, please." Olivia cringed. "We were sixteen, not sixty."

"Harsh. Anyway, just teasing, hon. And really, I'm over the whole club incident. After the initial panic when you disappeared, I asked around and the bartender said she saw you two go outside."

Olivia sighed. She could only explain what she'd felt as an all-consuming focus on Aerin whenever they were together, like nothing else mattered. It hadn't struck her as odd at the time, but the more she thought about it, the more she wondered if Aerin was capable of more than just mind-reading; perhaps she could influence as well. Really, though, Jody was probably right about her uneven feelings causing her to act strangely.

"Oh, I didn't tell you what happened the morning after."

Jody's eyes went wide. "What? What happened the morning after?"

"Geez, nothing like that. Get your mind out of the gutter. Actually, I ran into my mom. And the little brother I've never met."

Jody stood and squeezed Olivia's shoulders. "You saw your family? Oh my Lord, sweetie. How in the world are you feeling? And hello, how is Tuesday morning the first I'm hearing about this?"

"Oh, I mean, it was just like running into strangers. It's not like we have a relationship. The kid, though, he was cool. He liked my car." Olivia smirked.

"Hey, Dr. Perralta," Stanton said from the doorway. "Oh, Dr. Ando, didn't notice you there."

"No problem, come in. We're just taking a look at some test results." Olivia was eager to change the subject even though she'd brought it up.

Stanton walked into the room and sat in the chair next to her. He glanced at the papers haphazardly lined up on Jody's desk and blinked a few times. "What are these?"

"Brain waves. An electroencephalogram I did on—um, someone I know," Olivia said.

Stanton nodded. "They're supposed to be repeating patterns?"

"I guess they could be, technically, if someone was doing the same thing over and over without thought. But that's not what happened here. This spreads maybe a half hour. I doubt there would be patterns." Olivia gestured at the papers and reached toward the linoleum floor to lift up a stack that didn't fit onto the desk. "There are more."

"Can you lay them out, too? I'm definitely seeing patterns," said Stanton. Olivia looked at him skeptically and he doubled down. "Exact repeats. I'll show you."

They used the floor and some of the walls to hang the papers roughly sequentially. When they were done, Olivia looked around her. The room was covered completely in brainwaves, giving it an acid trip vibe. She had to close her eyes a few times to center herself as she examined them up close. No matter how hard she looked, she couldn't find any kind of repeating pattern. Then again, there were so many clustered brain waves on each sheet, the feat seemed impossible.

"See? Here, here and here. Oh, and over here. Same pattern. Then you see this repeating, too." Stanton pointed out each place he saw whatever he saw, but Olivia couldn't make out anything. She shot Jody a questioning look.

"He's really good at finding patterns that only computers can find. You know why?" Jody winked. Olivia knew what she would say, that brains were essentially computers, and she wouldn't give her that satisfaction. She chuckled and shook her head.

"Can I take a copy with me? If you look at it, it's like jazz music, rising and falling intervals. It's really interesting. The same patterns, but different notes. Different intonations. Same base. I want to play around with it."

Olivia shrugged. Whatever he saw, she certainly couldn't. "Sure, you can take this. I can always print more."

"Thanks. I'll be in touch." Stanton left with his armful of papers and Olivia gave Jody a look.

Jody shrugged. "Yeah, I don't know, either, but he's got a talent and he's always right. Anyway, I should prepare for class. Dinner later?"

"You know it," said Olivia, gathering up her things.

Olivia returned to her office to grade some tests from her morning class. Around four, she found her mind wandering to the lake. She had a feeling it would take being there to really understand the series of events that led Aerin to her. She had probably missed some big, obvious clue, something in her symptoms. Only one way to find out. It was time to do the background research that she'd been putting off.

She opened her computer, navigated to the university's library page, and entered Aerin's symptoms into the search box. Not many relevant results came up, but she wanted to be thorough, so she scanned every search result. Seizure, seizure, metabolic disorder, article after article. On the fifth page, she'd about given up when she came across an article from 1985 that caught her eye, "Erratic Brain Activity and Metabolic Disorder in Middle-Aged Man." She opened it and began to read.

"Oh my God. Oh my God. This is her. This is fucking her." Olivia skimmed the pages over and over. She printed the article and read it again, underlining the important points. Yes, erratic brain activity and weight loss. The man also claimed mind-reading abilities, which the author portrayed as indisputable fact. And there was the smoking gun, a lake, the same lake Aerin had been standing in when her incident occurred. This had to be more than just coincidence. Olivia grabbed her phone and called Aerin. Her excitement diminished ring by ring. By the time the voice mail picked up, she considered just calling back later. Telling the news to a machine was massively disappointing, but she ended up leaving a message asking Aerin to come see her later in the week.

For the rest of the day and through dinner with Jody, she kept her hand near her phone in case it buzzed. The usual after-work crowd filtered through the Green Leaf Café, creating a pleasant cacophony of small talk punctuated by sizzling vegan burgers on the grill.

Olivia hoped she'd blend into the background enough so that Jody wouldn't notice her distraction, but unsurprisingly, she noticed about halfway through their meal.

"What's up with you? Are you actually upset about seeing your family and are you willing to admit it?" She shoved a fry into her mouth and her face went orgasmic. "Mmm. How do they make these taste like my frigging dream food? God, yes. I need more." Jody ate another one and Olivia looked at her pointedly. "Sorry, it's just, these fries. What are you upset about?"

"You and the fries, every time. Anyway, I didn't mean to be so obvious. I'm just waiting for Aerin to get in touch."

Jody nodded. "Yeah? You're pretty antsy about it."

Olivia sighed. "I know. It's just weird that she hasn't responded yet. I called her about this article I found that seems like it fits with what's going on with her. She usually answers her phone right away, or texts me at least. I'm worried something happened to her, like maybe she actually had a seizure or something." Realizing just how worried she was the moment she said it out loud, Olivia broke into a cold sweat. She suddenly wanted to get into her car and drive to Aerin's house to check up on her, but that was crazy. Olivia didn't do things like that.

Jody began gathering their dishes to drop off at the bus stand. "Well, I can take a hint. I guess it is getting late, anyway. Better get back to the husband."

"Yeah, better get on the road. To my house, I mean." Olivia glanced at Jody, who gave her a strange look. No matter what she tried to tell herself about going home, her thoughts strayed back to Aerin. No, she should play with Mr. Piddles and watch her show before bed. She did the same thing every night, and wasn't that reason enough to keep doing it?

They walked out together, Olivia edging a little bit ahead, unable to shake the feeling of looming emergency. As she pulled onto the highway toward home, the sun had just begun to color the sky with brilliant pinks and oranges. Two of her favorite things about the plains were the incredible dusks and beautiful dawns. She was admiring the view when she realized she'd passed her exit. She considered turning around for a moment, but Aerin still hadn't called her and it was a nice night for a drive.

"I guess we're doing this. Aerin, you better be home. I do not drive to Tireville without a really fucking good reason."

CHAPTER TWENTY

Almost an hour later, Olivia pulled into Aerin's driveway. The house was easy to find again, just a few turns off the main drag on a wide suburban street. The solar-powered lights lining the walkway flickered as dusk encroached, but otherwise, the small brown ranch seemed unremarkable from the outside. Aerin's car sat in the driveway and a shadow passed behind a curtained window in the dim backlight. She wondered for a moment if Aerin might be seeing someone and if she might be interrupting them.

"Only one way to find out," Olivia said under her breath. She shut the car door loudly to make sure Aerin heard. On the porch, she hesitated before pressing the bell. After a moment, she didn't hear anyone moving around, so she rang it again. Still nothing. Shit, maybe she was on a date. Olivia stepped halfway down the front stairs so she could make a quick escape if she needed to. As she typed a text to Aerin, she saw movement from the corner of her eye. Aerin's confused face peeked around the living room curtain. Olivia gave her a small wave.

"Were you planning to knock, or just stand there like a creep?" Aerin asked as she opened the door.

"What do you mean? I rang your bell a couple times."

Aerin laughed softly, a slight blush coloring her cheeks. "Oh. Yeah, the bell doesn't work. I really should put a sign on it."

Olivia rolled her eyes. "Or, you know, get it fixed like a normal person. Can I come in?"

Aerin bit her lip and nodded, standing aside so Olivia could get by. Olivia met her eyes as she walked past. They were heavy and pink, as if she'd been crying, and Olivia felt an urge to gather Aerin in her arms and hold her there until everything was okay between them again. God, she must be tired. Maybe she should've gone home after all.

"So, what brings you here, Dr. Ando?" Aerin enunciated her title proudly, sending Olivia's stomach into a series of acrobatics.

"Can I sit?" she asked. Aerin nodded and followed her to the couch. Olivia was hyperaware of the small distance between them. She found it peculiar how she could be so drawn to someone she'd hated for so long.

"I found this." She thrust the paper at Aerin, hoping her flushed cheeks weren't obvious. "It's a journal article from the eighties and I think it has something to do with what you're going through." She sat back as Aerin pored over the text, twisting her wavy brown hair around her fingers. Olivia caught a hint of burnt sugar lotion and wondered if she were somehow hallucinating the smell again. Did Aerin seriously still wear the same kind of body lotion that Olivia had bought her all those years ago? She found her mind wandering to the car ride they'd taken together and the weight of Aerin's confession. What a cruel twist it was, after all these years, that Aerin was finally available and Olivia had put up walls.

She heard sniffling and looked up to see Aerin reading the paper with one hand over her mouth, silent tears rolling down her face. Olivia reached out and squeezed her shoulder. That small touch sent Aerin over the edge and she began sobbing into her palms.

"Hey, I'm sorry, I thought this could help us get to the bottom of it. I didn't mean to upset you," Olivia said gently. To her surprise, Aerin turned and embraced her.

"It's just everything, all at once." Olivia's suit jacket muffled Aerin's voice. Damn, she'd have to dry-clean it even sooner than normal. "Word got around that I'm a freak, so I lost almost all of my therapy clients this week. I just have a few online patients left." Olivia let her cry a little longer before carefully pushing her away.

Aerin held the paper up between them. "Did you even read this? It says the guy they interviewed was possessed by aliens." She tossed it back onto the coffee table. "Not the kind of fresh start I was hoping for after my divorce."

Olivia winced. "That's just what he thought. Anyway, at least we have some kind of lead. I don't know if it's possible, but maybe we can find this guy," she said.

Aerin sniffled. "He'd be really old. He's probably dead."

"Yeah. Only one way to find out." She used her phone to do a search on the paper's author. He was the head of the neuroscience department at a Canadian university. As she emailed him, her phone chimed with a message from Stanton, WAV file attached.

"Looks like Stanton found something in your EEG results."

Aerin cleared her throat and scrunched her eyebrows. "What? What's Stanton doing with my test results?"

Olivia blushed. Right, she shouldn't technically share them unless they were anonymized, but this was all under the table anyway. Besides, Stanton didn't know whose they were, unless he read the tiny print in the top right corner of each page. Okay yeah, maybe she should have tried harder. She ignored Aerin's question.

"I have no idea what's in this file, to be honest. But do you want to listen? It's about two minutes long."

Aerin nodded cautiously.

"Okay, here goes." She pushed Play and the piercing sounds of an alto sax filled the room. The melody sounded dissonant and choppy, but not unpleasant. Olivia could hear some of the repeating melodies Stanton had mentioned, though whether they were actually in the EEG readouts or not was up for debate. She turned to Aerin to gauge her reaction and found her with her hands over her ears, her face twisted into a silent scream.

Startled, Olivia fumbled the phone and it fell to the floor. She dove to grab it and knocked her knee against the corner of the table. "Fuck." She grasped the phone in one hand and her throbbing knee in the other. She had to jab the Pause button a few times before it finally shut off. The pain etched on Aerin's face tore her apart and she rushed to her, cradling her face.

"Aerin. Hey, Aerin?" She looked her over and met Aerin's darting eyes, blurred with panic, their focus on something beyond the room. Suddenly, they landed on Olivia's gaze, chilling her with their deep calmness.

"What's going on? Aerin, talk to me," she said. Aerin's intensity terrified her, but she seemed to be mentally present again.

"I—I can't. I don't know." Aerin's voice shook with vulnerability. "I saw something. God, I'm so tired. I think I need to go to bed." Her body withered as if all of her energy had simply vanished. She tried to stand without success.

Olivia's eyes darted around the room. Should she call

an ambulance? The second she considered it, the thought disappeared. Instead, she decided to take Aerin into the bedroom. "Here, let me help you."

Aerin leaned heavily on Olivia as they made their way down the hall, slowly. When they got to the bedroom, Aerin collapsed onto the bed, so weak that Olivia had to take her shoes off for her. Olivia doubled the blanket over her body and adjusted a pillow under her head. She knew it wasn't a good idea to stay the night, but the startling way Aerin had been affected by the music meant she couldn't exactly leave her alone.

Her ambivalence dissipated when Aerin looked at her with pleading eyes. Olivia could almost hear a voice in her head asking her to stay. She hated that she couldn't say no to Aerin after all these years, even after everything they'd been through. She hated that she didn't really want to.

"I'll sleep on the couch again," she said.

Aerin seemed to be nodding off already, murmuring something before she went still with sleep. Olivia watched her for a long, nostalgic moment, remembering how many times she'd watched her sleep like it was the simplest joy she'd ever know. As she turned off the light and started to shut the door, she heard a noise.

"Olivia? Thank you," Aerin said in a small voice. She gulped hard against the tenderness she felt and closed the door.

Back in the living room, she melted into the couch. If she had to be stuck on a desert island with only one piece of furniture, this damned amazing couch would be it. She switched the TV on to some show about killer whales that had snacked on various human extremities, but couldn't pay attention. Her thoughts kept wandering to a time when she would have climbed into bed with Aerin and held her all night.

It was dangerous to think that way with Aerin in the other room, with the possibility as near as it had ever been. It was unfortunately also highly arousing. After a while, she closed her eyes and gave in to the warmth of imaginary arms around her, hoping that if she stopped trying so hard to get Aerin out of her mind, she might finally disappear.

CHAPTER TWENTY-ONE

Olivia woke up on Aerin's couch at one thirty in the morning. Her shirt was damp with sweat and her head swirled. She'd had vivid sex dreams about Aerin since falling asleep, more accurately, a mixture of flashbacks and fantasies. Aerin naked against her, her body pressed into Olivia's crevices. Aerin kissing her neck, moving her hand over Olivia's thigh. God, she was so wet. It was the first time in years she'd felt the kind of desire she couldn't just wish away. She rose from the couch and made her way to the sink in the dim kitchen light, splashing her face with the coldest water she could get out of the faucet. The deep breaths she took as she leaned against the counter did nothing to slow her racing heart.

Suddenly, she heard a rustling in the hallway.

"Hey. Couldn't sleep?"

Olivia sucked in a breath. "Aerin. You're up." She tried to think of something, anything else. Aerin couldn't know about the smut circulating through her mind. She thought hard, baseball, shots at the doctor's office. Seeing her mother. That one did it; she finally felt the edge of her lust turn to panic.

"I had some weird dreams." Aerin crept forward with a darkness in her eyes. If Olivia hadn't already been imagining this moment, she'd have thought Aerin looked like a woman possessed. Aerin inched closer and she gulped hard.

"Huh. That's strange. Well, I think I'll just go back to sleep now," Olivia said. She looked everywhere but Aerin as she shuffled back to the couch. Please do not come over here, she thought. She watched Aerin take a glass out of the cupboard and fill it with water. She'd changed into a pair of sleep shorts and a thin T-shirt. Olivia could see far too much skin for her own good and she hardly had to imagine how full and gorgeous Aerin's breasts had become.

She shut her eyes, hoping that when she opened them again, she wouldn't have to make the choice between what she wanted as a human, a grown woman with desires she shouldn't have to hide, and what she should do as a professional researcher with boundaries. When she finally opened them, she found Aerin staring at her, mirroring her desire. Jesus, if she didn't get out of there, she'd definitely do something she would regret. She needed an excuse, any excuse.

"I just remembered that I have something to do tomorrow morning. Early. So, if you're okay, I'm going to go home." She didn't wait for a response as she leapt from the couch, carelessly gathering her things. As she slipped out the door, she turned back briefly and met Aerin's eyes. When she saw the need reflected in them, she knew she'd made the right decision.

CHAPTER TWENTY-TWO

Two loud thuds sounded from the foyer. Aerin hesitated, wondering who would stop by at such an early hour. She cautiously spit out her toothpaste, relishing the burn of the mint. It reminded her that some things hadn't changed, even if an alien was apparently taking up real estate in her brain. The knocking sounded again, heavy and hard.

Aerin wiped her mouth with the back of her hand and checked her hair. If Olivia was at the door, she wanted to look like she hadn't just rolled out of bed. Well, maybe a little like she had.

"Aerin, open up. I know you're in there. Don't make me late for work," said a muffled voice.

"Mom?" she shouted. Morning light filtered into the room through the edges of the living room shades. Meg had taught her that wasting bright sunlight was a crime, so she rolled the window coverings back to reveal a beautiful mid-morning glow, one she'd not seen for days.

"Aerin, are you there? I can hear you."

"Then why ask?" she mumbled. She opened the door to find a tired-looking Meg McLeary on her stoop. "Hi, Mom."

Meg kissed her cheek and came in. She smelled of fruity shampoo and coffee and Aerin remembered how nice it was to have her nearby, even if she rarely took advantage of the proximity.

Meg shed her outer sweater and placed it on the arm of the couch, the one Olivia had slept on, briefly, days before. "Honey, I'm going to be honest with you, and remember that I love you. People are talking, and you know I don't give a damn about them, but I'm worried. You haven't returned my calls for two weeks. What's going on with you?"

"I just—I'm going through some things at the moment. I'm fine, though. I promise."

Meg squeezed Aerin's bare arms and looked into her eyes. "Hmm. You're warm. Your pupils are dilated. Do you have a fever?"

Aerin shook her off, hugging herself. "I'm fine."

"Aerin, sweetie. I've known you your entire life and I can tell when something's wrong. And don't forget that I'm head nurse, so it's my job to know if something's wrong, especially with difficult cases like you."

"Oh my God, Mom. We all know you're head nurse. You don't have to bring it up every time."

Meg chuckled and poured herself a glass of water. "Just making sure you didn't forget." She absently primped her wavy brown-and-white peppered hair, pulled high in a tight bun. As far as mothers and daughters went, they looked oddly twin-like, which meant that either Meg looked young or Aerin had the face of an middle-aged woman.

"Is it Olivia? I heard she's back in town," Meg said carefully, raising her eyebrows.

Aerin let out a deep breath. She wasn't prepared to talk about Olivia right now, especially not with her mom. The details were too confusing. Although she knew she felt some kind of desire, she would never admit it. She changed the subject. "Mom, everyone thinks I'm crazy for divorcing Josh."

"You've been separated for months now, don't listen to them. Besides, he was all wrong for you," Meg said.

"Huh? I thought you liked him."

"I did. I just didn't think he was the one for you. He was fine as a person. You just never really loved him."

Aerin scoffed. "Uh, why didn't you tell me this earlier? You could have saved me years of my life and I could have found, you know, another person I liked better."

Meg set her glass down on the counter and covered Aerin's hand. "You already had a person you liked better. Anyway, I'm glad Olivia's in town. Maybe you two could come have dinner with me. I never get to see you anymore. I thought that with the divorce, you might spend some more time with me." She pouted and Aerin rolled her eyes.

"I'll come have dinner with you sometime this week, okay? Just me, though. Olivia has her own thing going on."

Meg smiled like she'd just won the lottery. "Good, good. I'll call you with the details. Answer your damn phone."

"I'll answer it. Or at least call you back within two weeks. Don't you have to get to work?"

Meg caught her eye and grinned. "Hmm. I do have to get to work, but you better believe we'll be continuing this conversation over dinner."

Aerin led Meg to the door and hugged her. "Bye, Mom."

"If you talk to Olivia, tell her I said hi."

"Bye, Mom," Aerin said again. She closed the door and sank to her knees.

CHAPTER TWENTY-THREE

"Woo, suck it, girl," Lindsay Nicole said as Aerin gulped her margarita through a penis straw. "One more day of freedom to suck as many penises as you want." They were in Indianapolis's trendiest bar for Aerin's bachelorette party. It was packed on this Saturday night.

Their waitress, Jamie, threw Aerin a sympathetic look from the end of the table while she delivered more drinks. Aerin smiled back, thankful that someone realized how ridiculous most of her wedding party was acting.

"That's not how it works, you dimwit," Zoe said. Lindsay Nicole's face fell, but she quickly recovered. Aerin's best friend and Josh's younger sister did not exactly get along, and apparently Zoe was too drunk to censor herself.

"Zoe, play nice. I have to be around this woman the rest of my life," Aerin whispered. Her mood darkened when she considered that yeah, she'd be getting married tomorrow and marriage was generally a thing that you were in until one of you died. "I'm going to run to the bathroom, okay?"

"Want me to come with?" Zoe asked. She preferred to hit the restrooms with a posse, a practice that Aerin could never understand. She considered it a more private experience, so she shook her head and got up.

She leaned hard against the porcelain sink and closed her eyes, dreading the minutes ticking by, her wedding closer with each one. The stall behind her opened and she heard footsteps approach the sink on the right.

"Hey, you okay?" the woman asked sweetly.

Aerin opened her eyes to find Jamie looking at her, eyes filled with concern. She had long dark hair so shiny and straight that Aerin wanted to touch it to confirm it was real. Around her hazel eyes was a faint ring of liner.

"I don't know what I'm doing," Aerin said softly, her head spinning with alcohol. She gripped the sink and squeezed her eyes shut, then looked up at Jamie. "I think I like girls, but I'm marrying a boy."

"Wow, that's a bummer," said Jamie.

"I think this is a mistake, but like, what else am I supposed to do? I can't not marry him. We've been together for years and everybody likes him. And then we get a waitress like you just reminding me of what I'm giving up." The alcohol apparently destroyed any shred of dignity Aerin had left, but what did it matter? She'd never see this woman again.

Jamie stared at her for a moment, considering. "Do you want to get out of here for a little?" Jamie asked. Aerin nodded and Jamie took her hand.

They exited the bathroom and slipped behind an Employees Only door, a storage room for extra alcohol and bar snacks. Jamie led her to a separate closet filled with glassware and locked the door. A small fluorescent light flickered overhead, casting them in a pale glow that reflected in the glasses.

Jamie leaned against the door, suddenly uncertain. "Is this okay?" She licked her lips and blushed.

"Yeah. This is good," Aerin said. She felt a fire in her belly that hadn't burned in years and closed the distance between them, crushing her lips against Jamie's in a searing kiss. This was the kind of kiss she'd been missing, full of heat and softness at the same time. Jamie's tongue brushed against her lips and Aerin moaned, fumbling with the zipper on Jamie's tight black pants, slipping her hand inside. She gasped as her fingers brushed the hot wetness soaking through. Jamie lifted Aerin's black sparkly dress, running her fingers across Aerin's stomach and then lower, to the place she needed it most.

"Oh, Jesus," Aerin said against Jamie's mouth. She felt like she might explode, so she moved Jamie's underwear aside and slid her fingers through her folds. At least they could come together. Their moaning became indistinguishable from the pounding in Aerin's head, until she steadied herself against Jamie's shoulder and shuddered hard. Jamie came a moment later and they just stood there, breathing heavily in the same space, Aerin miles away. She lifted her hand to her nose and inhaled, turned on all over again.

"I forgot how good this is. Can I see you again?" she asked.

Jamie wiped her hand on the inside of her pants and shrugged. "Sorry, I don't do this with married women. Just thought you were cute and wanted to give you a little sendoff."

"Oh, right." Aerin adjusted her dress and cleared her throat. "Thanks, then."

"My pleasure." Jamie kissed her once more, and it quickly turned into another heated makeout session. Aerin backed them into the corner and bumped the shelves. A glass shattered behind her, startling them both.

"I guess we should go. I've got tables that are probably wondering where the hell I am and you have to get back to sucking on those penises." Jamie smirked.

Aerin turned to glance at the broken pieces shimmering in the dull light behind them. She chuckled bitterly as they left.

Chapter Twenty-Four

O h my God, Olivia. Get out of my dreams." Aerin groaned as she rolled her face into the pillow, inhaling the comforting scent of her own sweat. It grounded her, helped her remember that dreams were sorely distant from reality. For the last week, ever since the night Olivia had shown up unexpectedly, Aerin had been dreaming about her. Olivia stroking her naked body. Olivia holding her during a lazy morning in bed, the sun bathing them in the impossibly bright light of a fantasy.

The look of panic in Olivia's eyes as they met in the kitchen in the middle of that night suggested she'd had similar thoughts. As she'd moved closer, she could hear Olivia trying to push the thoughts away.

She felt herself creeping into insanity between the Olivia dreams and the out-of-body experience she'd had from listening to Stanton's recording. The music had driven her mind to even stranger depths, moments she couldn't explain, time she'd lost. Aerin would descend into what she came to understand as conscious blackouts. She'd be driving or walking somewhere when the darkness took over. By the time she became aware again, her body had continued its path forward as if her mind had not just, for a fleeting moment, transcended everything she knew.

That first time, the day Olivia played the music, she saw things she couldn't describe. She'd slipped into another world, one so fantastical she thought she must be hallucinating. Confusion at first, then weightlessness as she zoomed past what looked like bright stars and ringed planets, clouds of gasses and bits of rock. It was like a video game of the universe that she played a few moments at a time, at least according to the clock. What she felt in there seemed like hours, years, millennia. If that other place contained the concept of time, it wasn't the time she knew. She wondered if the man from the article had also seen this place.

Her phone buzzed and she grabbed at the wooden nightstand for it. Eleven o'clock in the morning. Far too late for her to be sleeping in, but she didn't really have anything else to do except, you know, figure out how to pay the bills, maybe find a smaller house or apartment that she could afford. Wouldn't hurt to go on a date or two so she could feel things for someone besides Olivia.

Zoe had texted for the fifteenth time in two days. She felt guilty tossing the phone to the foot of the bed, message unread, but she couldn't deal with Zoe's hounding. She wanted to wallow alone, to not step outside the house until she felt good and ready, which could be ages. Aerin was prepared to dig in. She simply didn't have the energy to sort through the jumble of emotions she felt. She'd always been a better therapist than patient. As she sprawled across her queen-sized bed, she took a deep breath, reveling in the silence of the hour.

"Get up," she said to herself after some time had passed. She didn't seem to have heard herself, so she said it again. Finally, with enough coaxing, her body lifted from the bed as if it were a marionette. Lately, she'd been able to direct her body to move in certain ways or feel things it normally wouldn't. The other day, when she left the house with too many clothes on for the weather, she told her body to cool itself down. It had listened. Whatever had happened to her brain, at least there were some conveniences.

She grabbed her phone and shuffled down the hallway like a rag doll, a thin fog clouding her mind. Time for coffee and time to officially stop feeling sorry for myself, she thought. The automatic coffeemaker had shut itself off two hours ago and the liquid inside had cooled to room temperature. She poured herself a cup anyway and drank it black, savoring the bitterness as it settled on her tongue.

"Oh, I see. You are, are you?" she said as she read her messages. Zoe would apparently come over tonight to have a girls' night in. Well played. She'd been around long enough to know that it was a thinly veiled excuse to stage some kind of intervention. She vaguely wondered if people in town were talking about her closed therapy practice and financial problems. Of course they were. Her neighbors were the reason she'd lost her love years ago and they were the reason she was losing her livelihood now. She didn't like to admit it, but Zoe was part of the problem, right up there with the gossip rags. At least she didn't live right in town. Zoe had made it out, two whole towns closer to Indianapolis.

Aerin looked around and assessed the cleanliness of her house. Pretty dismal since she'd broken the lease on her office and moved everything to the living room. A pile of boxes sat near the front door, leaning precariously against the wall. The worn navy love seat had been too heavy to move by herself, so she'd left it. Anyway, it would have been a sorry reminder of a dream she had to give up. No use in opening her private practice in her own home, since she probably wouldn't be keeping the house with her meager income. Though the mortgage wasn't much, it was more than zero, which was about what she was bringing in. She felt her throat tighten as she considered what her next tiny dwelling would be like. She couldn't stay in Tireville. The town had effectively thrown her out and she didn't want to go crawling to her mother for help, even though Meg would do anything for her. That would seem like giving up for good.

Screw it. She was done with her own bullshit. Summoning an unfamiliar power, she got to work. Two hours later, she carried the last contractor bag of unnecessary belongings to the curb and wiped her brow. She felt clean and invigorated standing on her stoop and looking over the front lawn. One of her neighbors drove by, noticed the deluge of trash and scrunched his forehead. Screw you, she thought. So what if she only had two pans, three throws, and one tapestry left? How many pans did a single person need?

Her phone buzzed in her jeans pocket and she picked it up, rolling her eyes as she answered.

"Zoe. Hi."

"Hey, how are you feeling?" Aerin could hear the concern in Zoe's voice and scolded herself for not answering her texts.

"You don't have to worry about me, Zo. I'm okay. Just dealing with the fallout from that patient I had," Aerin said heavily. And so much more, she thought.

Zoe snorted. "Yeah, uh-huh. I know you too well, sweetheart. I'm coming over at seven tonight and we're going to fix all of your problems, okay?"

Aerin slid easily into the comfort of their friendship. Nothing she said would stop Zoe from coming over, and if she was honest, she wanted the company. "Yeah, okay. I'll see you later." She heard a car horn on Zoe's end and pinched the bridge of her nose to stave off the inevitable headache from its reverberation. "Are you driving?"

"No, I'm in Ben's basement. Wait, that sounds weird. I'm not being kidnapped, but I am in a man's basement. Do not send help."

Aerin laughed. "Okay. Later then."

Zoe showed up a half hour early with two subs and a bottle of wine. She shouldn't have bothered because Aerin still had about three bottles left from their trip.

"Love what you've done with the place. Is it that Japanese minimalism thing?" Zoe asked.

"No, it's the 'Aerin's sick of living like this' thing."

"So, all of your therapy people canceled on you." Zoe poured two glasses of red.

"Yeah, in a nutshell. I have a few online clients, but that's not very lucrative. I was barely making ends meet before and now there's no way." Aerin lay her head on the counter, suddenly drained. She needed to eat. "Give me a sandwich."

"Well, haven't lost your appetite, I see. Here." Zoe handed a sub over. "Now, listen to me. I have this crazy idea that could make you some money."

Aerin's mouth was full of half-chewed meatball sub. She didn't bother swallowing before she said, "No. No more ideas. Look how the last one turned out."

Zoe got into her begging stance, elbows on the counter, leaned in, hands clasped. "Just one more. Also, you can't say that you don't enjoy hanging out with Olivia. I saw you two at the show. You're welcome."

Aerin sighed. "Fine. What's your great idea this time?"

"You can read minds."

"That's not an idea. That's a fact," Aerin said.

"No, no, hear me out. You can hear what other people are thinking," Zoe said, stretching out the last word and widening her eyes.

Aerin took the hint. She concentrated and homed in

on Zoe's thoughts. "You're trying to tell me...oh. Oh." She opened her eyes and stared at Zoe. "That's brilliant. Screw it. Let's go." Aerin suddenly filled with energy, and she ran to grab her keys.

Zoe followed her, exasperated. "Wait, now?"

"Yeah, why not now?"

"Well, I mean, it is seven p.m. on a work night and we're going to have to drive about two hours to the nearest one." Zoe tried to reason with her, but Aerin was too amped to listen.

"I'm going. You can either come or not." Aerin grabbed a few bags of cheese crackers for the car and stuffed them into her purse.

"Oh, so that's how it's going to be. Jesus, Aerin, calm the fuck down and at least let me drive." Zoe rifled through Aerin's purse and pulled out the keys, holding them up triumphantly.

"Okay. You can drive. I'll set the GPS. Big River Casino, here comes one lucky poker player."

CHAPTER TWENTY-FIVE

The stale haze of cigarette smoke lingered in the parking lot like a warning. Aerin scrunched her nose at the acrid smell and took a deep breath, the last one she'd take for a while that consisted of mostly fresh air.

"You have everything?" Zoe asked. Aerin nodded as they walked hurriedly toward the casino entrance. Aerin could sense Zoe's nervousness as tension in her own body and tried to send her calming vibes. They would be fine. There was no way anybody would catch her cheating. Plus, was it actually cheating if she couldn't help her abilities?

"It's going to be fine. I bet we'll be in and out in less than an hour. Then I'm going to jump in the closest shower I can find and burn these goddamn clothes." Josh had turned her mild dislike of cigarettes into full-blown disgust every time he came back from a bar and tried to kiss her. It was bad enough without smoke and alcohol.

Zoe exaggerated a gag. "It's disgusting."

Inside the glass doors was a dimly lit lobby, almost completely empty. A faded red and blue carpet stretched down three hallways toward three different gambling experiences. Zoe crept closer to her and grabbed her arm for protection. This wouldn't be a fun night out, but Aerin needed the money.

"I think the poker tables are this way." Zoe pointed down a long corridor.

Aerin concentrated in that direction and heard the distant sound of shuffling. "Let's go. We have to look like we're enjoying it a little, though, or they'll know something's up. You could start by wiping that look of terror off your face," Aerin said.

Zoe grimaced. Aerin supposed that would have to do for now. For someone who'd come up with the idea to make quick money at a casino, Zoe was being a little too paranoid.

They chose a table with a few other players who looked like they were betting a lot but weren't very good. The dealer, Steve, was a fresh-faced young man who seemed like he'd rather be anywhere but the casino. Aerin listened to his thoughts for a moment. Her suspicions were confirmed. Steve wouldn't run to the manager if she won a few times more than the usual clientele.

She made an inquiring gesture toward an open seat and Steve nodded. Zoe stood behind her, arms crossed, trying to look mildly interested in the game. Aerin went through the steps in her head. Step one, she had to buy in. On the ride over, Zoe had made her read every online article she could find about how to play casino poker and she felt as ready as a complete newbie could be.

"Two hundred for me," she said to Steve. She slid over two crisp bills from Zoe's bank, where they'd stopped along the way for some cash. She was pretty sure she sounded smooth, like she had done this a million times before.

Steve nodded and slid a stack of chips in her direction. When she winked at him, he blushed, and she quickly glanced around to see if anybody else noticed. The other players were busy looking at Zoe. Between the two of them, most people were attracted to Zoe, and it wasn't as though the haggard men she was playing against were spoiled for choice. They probably couldn't believe two attractive women had come to their crappy little casino, let alone were playing poker with them.

The first hand was over quickly. Aerin didn't have decent cards, so she folded and used the opportunity to match the moves of the other players to what they were thinking. This wouldn't be difficult at all.

"Goddamn junk hand," one of the older men said. He'd stayed in for two betting rounds with a pair of fours. From what Aerin had read, this guy made a rookie mistake by disparaging his hand in a public way, revealing his tell.

The next two hands, Aerin batted her eyelashes as she pretended to think about her move. She knew they would fall for her stupid woman ploy, and they did. She was up several hundred dollars and riding the high when her phone buzzed. She played another hand, folding early. The phone buzzed three more times and she could no longer ignore it. What if someone really needed her?

Holding the phone under the table, she glanced at the messages. Just Olivia checking in on her. She put the phone away and stacked her chips, trying to disregard Olivia's concern. It kept creeping into her thoughts as she played a few more hands. What would Olivia think about this money making scheme? Though not exactly illegal, it was pretty obviously unethical.

Reality came crashing back and she looked up at Zoe, who eyed her hard. She'd seen the messages. *Do not go soft for her*, Zoe thought. *Think about Number One*. Aerin shuddered. What had this mob boss done with her best friend?

"Miss, are you in or out?" Steve was poised to deal the next hand. Aerin closed her eyes for a moment. One more, then they'd go. She nodded.

Two aces. After the flop, Aerin went all in. She could hear what everyone else had and it seemed like she would win this hand. The man across from her wore a tank top and a pair of tinted glasses. He squinted at her, trying to determine whether she was bluffing. She gulped and made sure to avoid his eyes. He took the bait. All in for him, too. The dealer turned over the third card. She had this.

She and the man across from her revealed their hands. She had two aces, surely the winning hand. She almost laughed out loud until she glanced at his cards. A pair of sixes, plus the six that had just been turned over in the community cards. The man winked behind his dirty glasses as the dealer slid the large pile of chips to him.

Aerin blinked, trying to read his expression, the confusion over losing all her money clouding her mind. Had he figured it out somehow? Did he know her secret? Was she just not that good at poker? She panicked, unable to control the influx of thoughts from the rest of the table. She looked wildly between the man and Steve, both unbothered by her loss. She didn't understand. She'd done everything right, how could she have lost? This wasn't working anymore. They had to get out of here before she was accused of cheating. Aerin thanked the dealer and slid him a five dollar bill, then grasped Zoe's elbow as they hightailed it out of the card room.

"What the fuck was that?" Zoe pulled her into an alcove. "Did he mind block you or something?"

Aerin's throat burned as she breathed hard. "I don't know. I think I misread the situation. I could read his hand, but I couldn't tell which cards in the deck Steve was going to flip. I hadn't thought of that. Damn it. I just lost a ton of money." Aerin knew it was more than just bad luck. She'd been distracted, thinking about how Olivia would react to her cheating at cards to make a quick buck. It had been so easy to justify. No harm done, winning the money from a casino, which surely had more than its share.

"I'm sorry, this was a bad idea," Zoe said, deflated.

Aerin shook her head. "No. God, I'm so stupid. What the hell was I thinking? Now I'm down two hundred bucks and I'm officially a cheater."

Zoe squeezed her shoulders. "Two hundred and five. No more ideas for either of us until we get all this sorted out, yeah?"

"Yeah. No more fast moneymaking schemes. Unless they're completely watertight."

CHAPTER TWENTY-SIX

Olivia's chair let out a long squeak as she leaned back and set her feet on the desk. The dim light from a desk lamp cast long shadows over tall piles of paper that she'd stacked around the edges. Her laptop halfway closed, she listened to a sound file on repeat through a pair of expensive noise-canceling headphones. It was the file Stanton sent, the same one that had driven Aerin into her nightmarish episode.

She must have listened to it twenty times, analyzing every note, every sequence, for some kind of clue. As hard as she tried, she heard nothing but the odd, off-key flights of Stanton's saxophone. The music sounded slightly eerie, comforting after she'd heard it over and over. In the end, though, she just heard the music, not whatever had disturbed Aerin. The only explanation she could think of was that Aerin processed way more information than just the music. There had to be some kind of hidden message that Olivia's brain was too primitive to hear.

She rubbed her temples and slipped the headphones around her neck so that the music played faintly against it. The only other noise came from the occasional popping and whooshing of the vents as the HVAC system switched on and off. It had been a while since she'd been at work this late and she remembered why she'd done it so often when she was first hired. It was the only time she could truly clear her mind.

The music sounded almost imperceptibly near her throat and she relaxed. A few minutes of sleep wouldn't be so bad, then she could drive home and deal with Mr. Piddles, probably already annoyed with her tardiness.

Olivia relaxed into the void between alertness and sleep, taking a few deep breaths to relax. Suddenly, she felt a pulling deep inside, as if her soul were being sucked out from her core. Alarmed, she tried to sit up, to stop falling toward the darkness, but she was paralyzed. Her heart beat frantically, pumping adrenaline through every inch of her body. She tried to scream but no sound came out. Then as quickly as it had started, everything went quiet. She saw nothing, heard nothing, smelled nothing. She couldn't feel herself as she tried to wiggle her fingers, and she became aware that she had no body. Maybe she'd never had one. It felt pure, natural, as if deep inside, her entire life, she had always been floating in the darkness, her soul immaterial. She floated now, weightless in the darkness of somewhere else that felt completely familiar. Eventually, she figured out the darkness was just her closed eyes, so she opened them. Points of light materialized around her, orbs of green, purple and yellow, translucent and solid. She floated past them and through them, soaking in their brilliance, feeling it inside her.

One orb of light in the distance drew her attention and she watched its yellow halo draw closer, drifting into an array of oranges and reds. As it came near, she felt the pulling toward the orb again, which began to resemble a fantastical version of Earth, vast marigold oceans and sunflower masses of land. Her fascination gave way to terror as she fell faster and faster toward the surface. She opened her mouth and tried to tell someone, anyone, that she would crash, but the only sound that came out was a whoosh of air.

Just as the waves' crests became visible and Olivia thought she would slam right into the orange ocean, she slipped back into her body and bolted forward, gasping for breath as if she'd been drowning. She gripped the arms of the chair for a moment to steady herself, then noticed the music from her headphones. She tore them off and threw them across the room. She had no idea what had just happened to her, but she couldn't deny that the music was the reason.

CHAPTER TWENTY-SEVEN

Olivia typed furiously on her laptop, desperate to record everything she could remember about the little vacation she'd just gone on. Her office felt tiny compared to the vast expanse of space she'd been thrown into, and she squirmed in her chair, trying to ground herself. She'd drunk the last sip of water from her mug ten minutes ago and wanted badly to fill it up again. She wouldn't, though, until she wrote everything down. If the experience was at all like what Aerin had been through when she'd heard the music, Olivia might be one step closer to putting the pieces together. And if she could see the same things Aerin had, perhaps that meant others wouldn't need to go through brain trauma to get their own minds to expand.

She needed to know exactly what had happened to Aerin when she heard the music, compare it to her own experience, and think on it. It was now after eleven, far too late to call without some kind of intimate pretext. Instead, she texted Aerin a poor representation of the wonder and terror that had occurred. Aerin called back almost immediately.

"Hey, what happened?" Aerin's voice calmed her racing heart.

"I, uh." She hesitated, aware that what she was about to say would make her sound insane to anyone outside this conversation. "I listened to the music. I don't even know what to call it, but it's like I went somewhere else."

"It's beautiful, isn't it?" Aerin said.

Olivia leaned forward until her elbows were on top of her desk. She couldn't have heard Aerin correctly. "Sorry, what? Didn't it cause you pain? Wait, did this happen again?"

She heard Aerin shift on the other end of the phone. "Well, yeah. A few times," she said.

"A few times?"

"All right, a couple times a day. Sometimes when I'm at home, sometimes when I'm in the car. I didn't tell you yet because it didn't seem like a big deal."

Olivia guffawed. "Jesus. You weren't even listening to the music those times. Aerin, if you want my help, you have to tell me everything," she said.

Aerin paused a moment. "Okay, noted. Won't happen again."

"Look, I think it might be best if you stay with Zoe for a little while. At least she can keep an eye on you and report to me what she sees. Ben can, too, if he's over." Olivia hoped Aerin wouldn't read too much into the real reason she wanted her to go to Zoe's. She was having what her father called "impure thoughts," and Aerin's closeness just made them worse.

"With Zoe? I don't know if she's really equipped to do that. I'm really fine by myself. I don't want to be an inconvenience."

Olivia sighed with regret. "You're not an inconvenience to anyone. I would have you stay at my house, but I just—I have a lot going on right now, and we need to know what's happening when you're going to that other place." She hoped Aerin couldn't read minds over the phone.

"Okay, I understand. I'll talk to Zoe."

"Thank you." Olivia was relieved. She wasn't sure why she cared so much that Aerin was safe, but she did, and it unnerved her. "I'm going to head home. I'll talk to you soon."

"Bye, Olivia."

"Bye."

As she hung up the phone, she noticed an unread email notification on the screen.

Dr. Ando,

I don't normally share information on my previous research subjects. However, this case in particular struck me, and for the last thirty years, I've not been able to get it out of my head. It is still a mystery to me, more confounding than any of the inner workings of the human brain, which I have studied for decades. If I am able to track the man down, please assure me that you'll share whatever you find about your subject.

Cordially, Max Pelletier

The lateness of the hour, her jolting experience floating through space, and this piece of good news broke Olivia. She bent into her arms and cradled herself as she wept. She hadn't cried this much since Aerin had run out of the church a decade and a half ago, and it was cathartic. Finally, she was out of energy to cry, so she wiped her nose as her gut rumbled with emptiness. It was time to go home.

CHAPTER TWENTY-EIGHT

Late Sunday evening, as the sun cast the living room in golden hues, Aerin packed a small bag for Zoe's. She'd just added her toothbrush and was about to grab her keys when she heard a knock on the door. Thinking it must be an unplanned lift from Zoe or Ben, she opened it without her usual glance out the window.

She went numb when she saw who was at the door. Josh stood on the stoop next to Pastor Ando. Aerin stared at them, looking from one to the other, trying to quickly pick up on their motives before she slammed the door in their faces. There was a lot going on in their minds. Josh had heard she'd gone crazy and thought that whatever they were about to do would help. Plus, a small part of him wanted revenge for his apparent humiliation at having someone divorce him. Pastor Ando seemed to be in an even darker place, convinced it was his duty to save Aerin from her sins. Great, an exorcism.

Before she could close the door and get on with her night, Josh stuck his arm out to catch it.

"We'd like to talk," he said evenly.

Aerin's heart raced with a hefty flow of adrenaline. "You know, I'm actually on my way out." She grabbed the edge of the door and tried to push it shut, but Josh was too strong. He held it open easily and even seemed to smirk. She felt them advance toward her, even though they didn't move. Suddenly light-headed, she stumbled backward into the kitchen to grab the phone she'd left charging. If she was fast enough, she'd be able to shoot off a text before they realized what was going on. Maybe someone would come and save her before the pastor tried to.

Her hands shook as she unplugged the phone and typed a message to Zoe. She'd almost hit Send when Pastor Ando gently, firmly, removed the device from her hands.

"Aerin, we'd like to talk to you." He slid the phone into his pants pocket. "We're worried about you. We think you might have some darkness inside you."

"Josh, please tell him to leave," she shouted. If anybody was going to be on her side, it would be her ex. He wasn't a bad person. He usually had morals, but the pastor must have convinced him to shove them aside for this visit.

Josh walked over and stood behind Pastor Ando. "Aerin, we're just concerned. First, you don't want me anymore. We're talking about me, the guy who's been there for you since high school. I don't believe you just lost interest. I think there's something else going on."

"Josh, I never loved you. There wasn't anything else going on. Now, please leave."

He shook his head and continued. "You're acting weird. Everyone heard what happened with the pervert at your office. And don't think we weren't aware Olivia's back in town, staying over at your house. You're sick, Aerin. We're trying to make you better."

Aerin burned hot with anger. She groped the countertop behind her, fingers grazing the knife block. Deftly, she pulled the cleaver from its slot. By the time the pastor realized what was going on, she was waving it in his face. Her breath came in short spurts and she could almost taste Pastor Ando's sudden fear.

"I do not give a damn what you two think of me, or anyone else in this godforsaken place. Get. The. Hell. Out. Both of you," she said quietly, willing them to leave with all her might.

"Okay. Okay." The pastor put his hands in the air, too easily. "I can tell that we caught you at a bad time."

Aerin scoffed. "No, there's never a good time, you insane cult leader. You barged into my house." She turned to Josh. "My house, Josh. Not yours anymore. I believe that's called breaking and entering, and that's a crime. There's nothing wrong with me. Give me my phone and get the hell out."

Pastor Ando threw her phone on the counter and it struck the edge of the sink, shattering the screen. When he saw what he'd done, he backed away and rushed Josh out the door.

"Don't come back," she yelled after them. A green Civic slowed in front of the house to watch the two grown men running like rabbits from Aerin's front door. Aerin caught the onlooker's eye and flipped him off before he sped away.

She closed the door and leaned against it hard until she heard the sound of the pastor's engine starting. Then she paced the living room, torn between hightailing it to Zoe's and calling the cops to report the incident. Reporting a pedophile was one thing, an assault that hadn't left any bruises quite another. She picked up the phone to call the police, then set it down. The cops were churchgoers, friends with Josh, town boys. If they took her seriously, that would be a miracle in itself.

She'd just have to be more diligent with security and maybe, once things settled down, figure out how to get the heck out of Tireville. She locked the door on the way out, got into her car, and sped down the road to Zoe's house. She'd decide later whether to tell anyone, but for now, it looked like she could fend for herself.

Chapter Twenty-Nine

"Come on in," Olivia said. Ben cracked her office door and peeked in, then opened it all the way.

"Hey. Thought we should check in about Aerin since it's been a few days."

"How's she doing?" Olivia shifted in her chair so the late afternoon sun wasn't in her eyes.

Ben shrugged. "Okay, I guess. She seems mostly fine, but then sometimes she zones out a little. It's weird, though, because she'll be making a sandwich or something, then she'll start humming and she's still making the sandwich. When we call her name, she doesn't answer. It's creepy, like she's possessed."

"So, not okay."

Ben chuckled. "Fine, not okay. I'm not sure what else you want me or Zoe to do for her. It does seem like she can take care of herself just fine. Besides, with Dad still in recovery, it's not really the best time for either of us to have to worry about someone else."

Olivia nodded. "Send me your parents' address again. I want to send over another couple of breakfast bakes."

He smiled. "They really liked those. Thanks. I will."

They sat in silence for a moment, Olivia chewing the

inside of her lip. She had a feeling that sending Aerin to stay with Zoe and Ben was only deferring the inevitable. She shouldn't have hoisted her problems onto her friend in the first place.

"Everything okay?" Ben asked.

Olivia shook her head. "I don't know. I should probably just get Aerin to stay with me and do some more tests." She let the end of the sentence hang between them.

"But you're in love with her and don't want things to get complicated?"

Olivia's eyes snapped to his. "What?" she asked sharply.

Ben recoiled. "Oh, sorry, is that not public knowledge? Zoe told me."

Olivia's stomach sank. "I barely know Zoe. How would she know if that's what I was thinking? Which I'm not," she said pointedly.

Ben thought for a moment. "Maybe Aerin said something to her? I'm not entirely sure, to tell you the truth."

So, Aerin saw right through her. Great. That should make continuing to work together a treat.

"This world feels way too small sometimes," she said.

"I hear you. I ran into my ex at a coffee shop the other day and we had a moment. Not a good one."

"Charlotte?" Olivia asked. She'd only met her once, and the amount of time Charlotte had spent flirting with her made it clear that the Charlotte-Ben combo was not a match made in heaven.

"Brit. She was before I knew you. Killer in the sack, but possibly an actual killer in real life. When I broke up with her, she followed me around for weeks trying to tell me I was the One," Ben said.

Olivia laughed. "Glad you got out of that relationship before it was too late."

Ben sighed. "So? You and Aerin? She's gorgeous, she has a great sense of humor, and did I mention she's gorgeous?"

"Didn't Zoe tell you anything about our history?"

Ben leaned in and put his forearms on the table, like he wanted to make a point. "Yeah, but that was high school. This is real life. This is where things get good. You weren't going to make it if you stayed together back then. You would have left for college and moved on. You're kind of lucky, actually. You get a second chance."

Olivia huffed. Lucky? She felt the opposite, whatever that was. "Ben, I hate to break it to you, buddy, but there are no do-overs in life. It just is what it is."

Ben shrugged, resigned to let Olivia be stubborn. "Well, those are just my two cents. I want you to be happy, and Aerin seems like a great person, despite what may have happened to you a lot of years ago."

"Keep dreaming. When you get to Zoe's, send Aerin to my place, okay? And make it very, very clear that there's nothing personal about it."

Chapter Thirty

The fire was dying down as Olivia, Aerin, and twelve other members of the Tireville Baptist Youth Group sat cross-legged in the dark. Most of them bowed their heads in prayer. The occasional pop of sparks made the orange glow dance across their faces. Olivia was exhausted from hiking all day and anxious to get back to the tent she shared with Aerin. Lately, she'd been looking forward to the time they spent together more and more, and tonight was no exception.

They'd been friends since third grade, and now that they were fifteen, Olivia knew almost everything there was to know about Aerin. She knew her favorite color was blue and that she could never decide what to have for lunch but eventually always settled on the same thing, a peanut butter sandwich without the jelly. She couldn't have asked for a better best friend. Aerin made everything about her life, including these youth group outings, bearable.

A hand on the small of her back sent shivers up her spine.

"Hey, I'm ready to turn in. Do you want to come?" Aerin whispered.

Olivia nodded energetically, tired of prayer time. She had enough of that every day of her life, at home and at church on Sundays, which were nonnegotiable, according to her father.

They crept away from the prayer circle without drawing attention. Olivia unzipped the tent and let Aerin climb in first. Aerin smelled like an intoxicating combination of burning wood and sweet body wash. Olivia swooned before remembering this was her best friend and she definitely wasn't supposed to feel this way about any girl ever. They sat on their sleeping bags, facing each other, and she thought about her father at the lectern, preaching about eternal damnation or the sin of the week. The image sobered her racing heart for a moment.

"Want to come here and lie next to me?" Aerin asked. This was what they did when they spent the night at each other's houses. They'd go to sleep cuddled against one another, and Olivia usually found it comforting. Lately, though, it had been distracting her from actually sleeping.

"Do you think this is a good idea? What if someone sees us and thinks something weird is going on?"

"Trust me," Aerin said. Olivia could hear her breathe, amplified in the small space. "Nobody will see us. And nothing weird is going on, silly."

Olivia wasn't so sure, especially with only a thin piece of fabric between them and the rest of the group. She didn't want to say no to Aerin, though, so she slid against her body and rested her head on Aerin's arm. She closed her eyes as Aerin turned toward her, pretending she was anywhere but here, the only place she really wanted to be. She could feel herself being pulled further into reality with each pass of Aerin's hand across her stomach. Aerin had recently started to touch Olivia innocently in stolen moments, rubbing her arm, touching her back, grazing her stomach. Olivia never said anything because best friends did that, right? Besides, she enjoyed it too much. She was the one who was taking a simple gesture and letting it drive her completely insane. It was all her fault.

"Hey, your heart's beating fast." Aerin chuckled. "I can hear it." She removed her hand from Olivia's belly and placed it over her chest. Olivia just about died and drew in a hard breath. She tried to even out her breathing, but she sounded like she'd just run a marathon. She hoped to God Aerin didn't realize what was happening to her.

"How come it's beating so fast?"

Olivia wanted to cry with frustration. What could she say that wouldn't risk losing her best friend? Besides, she wasn't exactly sure why Aerin made her feel this way. She just did and it sucked.

Then Aerin did something unexpected and terrifying. She leaned over and kissed Olivia's cheek, holding her lips there long enough for Olivia to get the hint. When Aerin pulled away, Olivia turned to her. She could barely make out the terrified expression on Aerin's face, but she felt the fear between them, like a wall that grew higher every second she waited. Finally, she couldn't stand it any longer and she kissed Aerin on the lips the way Jack kissed Rose. She felt the relief in Aerin's hands as they tentatively explored her skin.

After a while, lips tender and swollen, they stopped and lay next to each other. Olivia's eyes darted back and forth, searching for something in the dark fabric of the tent that might confirm she was awake. Aerin took her hand and squeezed it.

"Can we do that some more?" Aerin asked. Olivia let out a strangled laugh. What a question. She wanted more of it, all of it, but she didn't know where to start. She nodded.

Aerin rolled onto her elbow and pressed her lips into Olivia's neck. A soft moan escaped Olivia's mouth and she covered it with a corner of her sleeping bag. Aerin swirled her fingers along Olivia's torso and brought them to her breast.

"Can I?"

Olivia nodded again, driven by need she'd never

imagined. She felt Aerin's breath against her neck as she stared through the dark toward the tent ceiling. She almost passed out when Aerin's finger moved over her nipple, seduced by the manifestation of her most forbidden fantasy, and the surprised sound that Aerin made against her neck. Before tonight, she wasn't sure that Aerin had been touching her on purpose; now there was no doubt.

Olivia didn't want Aerin to stop and she didn't want to know what would happen if she continued. Where was the point of no return? Had it already been passed? Aerin slid her hand down Olivia's sweatpants before she could figure it out. Sparks exploded behind her eyes at Aerin's touch and she saw static above her, matched by the fire between her thighs. That she was now having sex with her best friend didn't make sense if she thought too much about it, but when she stopped thinking, she knew that deep down it was what she'd always wanted.

Aerin rolled on top of her and buried her face in Olivia's neck, biting it gently. They kissed some more and Olivia moaned, losing track of the moments passing, focusing on Aerin's breath, hot and heavy in the small tent. The smell of wood smoke and sweat overwhelmed her as Aerin moved her fingers over and over, tightening the knot below Olivia's stomach until it broke free in a strangled cry. Aerin obscured the sound with her mouth as it happened, their tongues pressing against one another. After Olivia was done, Aerin pressed her lips to her cheek, a simple gesture that slowly brought her back to earth, back to the tent and Aerin's hand that now rested on Olivia's shirt.

She breathed into the darkness as her body adjusted to its new possibilities, all of them disturbingly far from what her father would expect. Olivia felt Aerin pick up her hand and wipe it on her own pants. She wasn't sure if she should say something, or kiss Aerin again, or do what she'd just done to her. Nothing made sense, but a small part of her world finally fell into place. Aerin shifted slightly so she could hold Olivia's hand and lay heavily on her shoulder.

"Was that weird?" Aerin whispered.

Olivia couldn't find words. She wanted to laugh and cry, scream at Aerin, demanding to know what in the world had just happened between them. She felt Aerin shaking against her, could almost taste the fear that she'd ruined something precious. She kissed Aerin on the forehead to let her know she hadn't ruined anything. Maybe she'd begun building something better.

Aerin cleared her throat. "Was it okay?"

Olivia nodded, even as she rolled the word "okay" over her tongue, trying desperately to figure out what it meant.

CHAPTER THIRTY-ONE

Aerin was slouching on Olivia's doorstep when she returned from work that night. She gave a small wave as she pulled into the driveway. Olivia took an extra few moments to gather her things before going inside.

Despite her repeated insistence that nothing romantic existed between them, Olivia nervously paced the kitchen while Aerin was in the bathroom. She wrung her hands and ran them through her hair, forcing a few deep breaths as she heard the sink running. Aerin emerged looking even better than Olivia could remember, shyly smiling and blushing. Right. Because she could hear Olivia's internal monologue. She forced herself to think of her students' final papers, which she'd been grading that afternoon.

Aerin leaned a hip against the island and crossed her arms. "I'll probably head to bed soon. Should I take the couch?"

Olivia blanked for a moment. "Uh, the couch, yeah." She shifted ever so slightly away from Aerin. "I set my phone to alert me if there's any deviation from your normal brain wave patterns in case I fall asleep later. Otherwise, I'll stay up as long as I can to observe the readings and any behavioral changes."

Aerin raised her eyebrows. "You'll be watching me sleep?"

Olivia burned bright red. "No, no. I have papers to grade, so I'll be up anyway. Just in case something happens. Also, it's barely seven thirty. I don't go to bed until ten." She watched Aerin's face soften in amusement.

"I am really hungry. I usually eat another meal before bed. Do you have anything?" Aerin asked. Before Olivia could answer, Aerin got up and opened the fridge.

"Find anything interesting?" Olivia asked. She didn't keep much at home except the essentials, and since she didn't do well with variety, there wasn't much there.

Aerin shrugged, closing the door. "Do you have anything breakfasty? Pancake mix? Oatmeal?"

"Oatmeal. I do have that. How many packets do you want?"

"How many packets do you have?" Aerin asked suggestively, sliding along the countertop. Only Aerin could make oatmeal sexy.

Olivia ignored her as best she could. "Six or so."

"Can I have all of them? Don't look at me like that. I have a metabolism problem."

Olivia gave her the entire box of oatmeal packets and flinched as she put them all in a pot with some water. "It's a variety pack, you know. It might taste weird all together," she said.

"I don't care. Honestly, I'm so sick of being hungry all the time. I'll eat practically anything." Aerin stirred the contents together as apple-maple-raisin-scented steam rose from the pot. It actually smelled pretty good. "I'll save you a bowl." Aerin winked at her.

Olivia just shook her head and rolled her eyes. "Is there any chance that we can ever be in the same room and I'll be able to have my own private thoughts?"

"Maybe when I'm sleeping? You'll have to find out and

let me know. It's pretty exhausting listening to everyone else's thoughts all the time." She shrugged.

"Oh, I hadn't thought of that," Olivia said sheepishly.

Aerin just nodded and dished out the oatmeal. Olivia found two spoons in the clean dishwasher. "I hardly ever empty it. I don't go through that many dishes by myself," she said.

Aerin blew on a spoonful of oatmeal. "I get it. Since Josh left, I've had to figure out how to cook for one. And then since this happened, I've been quadrupling my recipes. Still only use so many dishes, though, so I usually just rinse them in warm water and use them again."

"Really sanitary," Olivia said and they both laughed. The mood in the room lightened as they looked at each other for a long moment. Olivia looked away first, concentrating on the piping-hot bowl in front of her. Hungrier than she realized, she barely waited for the oatmeal to cool down before scarfing it down in an alarmingly rude fashion.

"Sorry," she said.

Aerin had a ways to go, but Olivia wasn't going to wait around for her. She didn't trust herself. "I'm getting ready for bed, and then we can hook you up so you can go to sleep." She yawned and squeezed her eyes shut. Why was she so tired? "I may not be grading papers after all."

"Suit yourself," Aerin said.

Olivia put on pajamas and returned to find Aerin already on the couch, elbows on her knees, humming quietly. She rocked back and forth in a slow rhythm, her vacant eyes fixed on something in front of her.

"Aerin?" Olivia called cautiously. "Aerin?" No response. This must be the zoning out that Ben had mentioned. Aerin was in some kind of trance Olivia wouldn't be able to break, singing an odd, dissonant tune. She quietly retrieved her phone from the kitchen counter and set it to record. She needed to know whether the song was the result of the trance or had somehow caused it. Maybe she could find out by playing it back to Aerin when she woke up.

A moment later, Aerin snapped out of her trance as if nothing had happened. "So, the sleep helmet?"

Olivia walked over to the couch. "Do you know you just went into a trance?"

"A trance? Huh. I didn't realize that's what happens."

Olivia nodded. "What did you think happens?"

Looking at her hands, Aerin shrugged. "Honestly? No idea. I'm so enthralled by what's going on in my mind that I haven't thought too much about it."

"There was a song, too. You were humming." Olivia almost showed her the video on the phone, but she thought back to the music Stanton had sent. It probably wasn't a good idea to risk a repeat performance right now. There would be time tomorrow.

Aerin watched her for a moment, listening. "I'm curious, but if you don't think it's a good idea, I'll wait."

Olivia hid her exasperation and went to get the helmet. She fastened it on Aerin's head, avoiding breathing her in too deeply. She set a few blankets on the coffee table.

"Feel free to wake me up if you need anything, okay?" Olivia hoped Aerin wouldn't take her up on the offer.

"You too," Aerin said evenly.

Olivia felt a rush of heat. She had a feeling sleeping would be difficult. She couldn't even let herself think about the way it made her heart race when Aerin was nearby. Aerin apparently already knew too much about how, against her better judgment, Olivia wanted her.

She left the living room quickly, taking the stairs in twos and closing the door to her room. She wished she'd had the foresight to cover the walls in tin foil or attach the room to a rocket that would propel her far enough away from Aerin that she could properly examine her dirty thoughts. To distract herself, she opened the app and watched the brain waves recording. Nothing out of the ordinary, for Aerin at least. God, she could use a good evening alone with her vibrator, long forgotten at the bottom of her nightstand drawer. Even five minutes would do the trick, but she wasn't about to get Aerin all hot and heavy via ESP. "Baseball, your mom, your brother, your asshole father. Your asshole father." Yup, that worked. She was now thoroughly uninterested in sex and quite annoyed at her estranged family.

Once her head hit the pillow, Olivia fell asleep. She slept soundly until three forty-five a.m., when her phone started buzzing.

She grabbed for the phone to decline the call. "Who the fuck is calling me?" she muttered. She'd almost silenced the phone when she realized the noise was the app alerting her to a change in Aerin's brain activity. She bolted upright and looked at the real-time output. It was indeed a different pattern than she'd seen, bursts of activity punctuated by moments of silence in between.

Throwing the blankets off, she quickly made her way downstairs to the living room, giving her eyes a few moments to adjust to the darkness. She couldn't see Aerin, so she blinked hard, willing the visual purple to work faster. It wasn't her eyes that were the problem, though. Aerin was gone.

"Shit," she whispered. Her keys were on their usual hook by the door and she grabbed them for the small LED flashlight keychain. She used it to illuminate her way around the house, checking the entire floor for Aerin. Mr. Piddles squawked when she popped her head into his room, but she had to break it to him that they weren't going to have a midnight play date. She hadn't heard Aerin come upstairs, which left only one area: the basement, where she stored all of her expensive precision equipment.

She tiptoed down the carpeted stairs, careful not to alarm Aerin if she was indeed down there. When she hit the bottom step, she looked around. At first, nothing seemed out of the ordinary, but as she listened, she heard a series of clicks. In the far corner, she made out the soft glow of a computer. As she moved closer, careful not to trip over any wires, she saw Aerin staring at a desktop screen, typing some kind of computer code syntax that Olivia hadn't seen before.

She called Aerin's name softly, hoping that she'd just wandered down here because she was awake and bored. She waited a moment for a response, but there wasn't any. Olivia's phone showed the same patterns that had triggered the alarm. Standing right next to her, she watched Aerin bring up message after message in some kind of ancient-looking internet forum. Olivia typed the beginning of the URL into her phone's browser and brought up a list of bulletin board systems. The term sounded vaguely familiar, probably something Jody had mentioned in passing. Whatever they were, Aerin seemed to know how to access one of them.

As the messages scrolled by, Olivia did her best to pick out words she could identify. They didn't make sense until Aerin stopped scrolling. The post she'd landed on chilled Olivia to the bone. Its author was Max Pelletier, dated 1981, four years before he would have published the paper Olivia found. She brought up her phone's camera, turned the flash off, and took a picture of the post.

Send to user: HANSDOC
TITLE: Need Your Help
DATE: 11/12/81 21:40

Hans, thank you for the well-wishes. I have passed them on to Eleanor and she is also appreciative. I need to ask your advice, as a doctor and as a friend. I've run into a strange case that warrants some investigating. Perhaps you should ring me. It's very sensitive.

Max Pelletier

Aerin scrolled through several more exchanges, stopping quickly to read each one. Olivia took photos of them, skimming them each time Aerin began to scroll again.

Replying to: MAX1MILLION
TITLE: Re: Need Your Help
DATE: 11/14/81 21:18
Dear Max,

I apologize again for not answering your call until this evening. I've thought of some other questions for the gentleman in question since we spoke. Aside from doing your due diligence in getting a full history, I believe it's most important to understand the moments preceding and following the incident. I understand that he was vague in his recollection, but you must pull it out of him. Perhaps try a hypnosis session? I will be away again for the next three days. If you need to reach me, the hotel information will be in the next packet.

Hans Schilling

Send to user: HANSDOC
TITLE: Re:Re: Need Your Help
DATE: 11/18/81 03:22

Hans, please call when you return. I met with the man in question today with interesting results. You will recall that he insists he is possessed by some kind of dark energy. His Jewish upbringing would not suggest to me an ingrained belief in spirit possession, but then again, I am not well versed in the matter. As for the questions regarding the moments before and after the incident, I was planning to ask him (I had written it down on my pad), but the strangest thing happened. I simply skipped over them as though they were not there. I only realized it after he'd left. Instead of discussing the incident in our meeting, he proceeded to tell me a fantastical story I cannot attribute to anything but an active imagination. I won't bother recounting it here, though perhaps I will on the phone, if you're in need of a good laugh.
Max Pelletier

Olivia's phone went to sleep while she examined the last picture she'd taken, and she scrambled as Aerin moved on to another reply. She quickly swiped the camera and took another picture without disabling the flash. The bright light bathed the room in a pale wash and she stepped back in alarm. She lost her balance and fell into an old hospital bed, which crashed against the wall. Aerin gasped and muttered something she couldn't make out.

From her half-fallen position, Olivia watched as Aerin stood and stepped away from the computer in shock. "What the hell? Where am I? What is this place?"

In the dim glow, Olivia watched her look wildly around the room. "Aerin, I'm over here. Calm down, okay? You're safe." Olivia stood and grabbed Aerin's bare elbow.

"What is this? Are they gone? Please tell me it's over." Aerin's eyes were wide and a deep crease marked her forehead.

"Aerin, what are you talking about?"

To her surprise, Aerin fell into her arms and hugged her tightly around the waist. Olivia didn't respond until she realized Aerin's tears were soaking through her thin T-shirt. What was the deal with Aerin using her as a human tissue? She tentatively put her arms around Aerin's back and held her. A million forgotten feelings surfaced as she buried her nose in Aerin's soft hair and held on dearly. She thought about what Ben had said about giving Aerin another chance, and for the first time, she considered his wisdom.

Aerin's voice sounded muffled against Olivia's shoulder. "There was a bomb. I couldn't stop it."

Olivia let Aerin go and looked at her. "Did you dream about a bomb?"

Aerin nodded. "It was bad. A lot of people died. They drowned right in front of me."

She took Aerin's hand and squeezed it. "It sounds like you just had a nightmare. Let's go back upstairs."

"I don't want to go back to sleep," Aerin whispered. Olivia drew a harsh breath, unprepared to resist Aerin's advances. "I'm scared. I think I'll watch TV instead."

Thank God, Olivia thought. Her willpower was paper-thin tonight, it wouldn't take more than a nudge to break through. She lit the steps with her small flashlight as they returned upstairs. There was nothing on the DVR but *Sunrise Lane*, so Olivia set it to play from the beginning of the season. As she fell into bed again, she remembered the last photo she'd taken, the one with the flash. The picture was marred with a reflection of Aerin's distant expression, but she could make out most of the text.

Send to user: MAX1MILLION
TITLE: Some Thoughts
DATE: 11/25/81 20:25
Dear Max,
   It has been a week since we talked on the phone, and a week since I had a moment without thoughts swirling through my head. I know you believe your patient's story to be farcical, but I cannot help wonder. What if he is indeed possessed by a spirit from a distant universe? What does it want with Earthlings? I believe you should pursue this possibility until it can be disproved.
   Hans Schilling

Olivia reread the message a dozen times, analyzing the clear delusion on the subject's part. Regardless, she lay awake until the sun rose, Hans's words echoing in her mind.

CHAPTER THIRTY-TWO

The pile of papers waiting to be graded mocked Olivia. She'd been at work for two hours, checked up on Aerin five times, and had to prepare for an NPR interview at one. None of this affected her lack of motivation to get the students' grades in by the deadline at the end of the night. She couldn't stop thinking about Max's case study subject and the suggestion that a being had possessed him from a distant universe. The moment she'd read it, she dismissed it as ridiculous, baseless, and way too convenient. But Max had published it in a journal that, while not the top in their field, was known for publishing legitimate case studies. A small part of her wondered how far-fetched it really was.

She rubbed her eyes, dry from the hours spent staring at her dark ceiling this morning, and checked her phone. More than anything, she wanted an email back from Max with information about his research subject. And after last night, she had some further questions for him. Her inbox showed a new message, and she clicked on it without looking at the sender.

"Oh, shit," she murmured. The sender was homeboy208@gmail.com, and she was certain she'd just clicked on spam. Then she saw the signature: Emmanuel. Her little brother had sent her an email. From an email address called homeboy208. She chuckled.

Dear Olivia,

I'm glad I got to meet you. I'm not supposed to write to you, but Mom and Dad don't know about this email account, so it's cool. I think it's dumb that they kicked you out for being gay. I found that out from one of my friends who has an older brother. I was wondering if I could come and visit you sometime? I looked up your address so I know where you live and it's not that far. Plus, your job sounds cool. I mostly like science and math, too. Can I come and visit you when school's out in a couple weeks? I can tell Mom and Dad that I'm somewhere else.

Please let me come!
Sincerely,
Emmanuel

"God, could my life get any more fucked up?"

"Someone say something about getting fucked up?" Jody popped her head into Olivia's office with a giant grin. "Gary got us a little weed the other day. I may or may not have a tiny bit in my car right now."

Olivia moaned. "Jody, I'm drowning. There's not even time to give you all the details, but I can tell you that I just got an email from my little brother."

Jody sat down with rapt attention. "And?"

"And he wants to visit me, but obviously that cannot and will not happen." Olivia folded her arms and leaned back in her chair.

"You think you'll get in trouble?"

Olivia nodded. "For sure. If they find out, they'll probably accuse me of kidnapping him, which is absurd, but they're absurd people."

"What if you happened to run into him somewhere? That would be okay, wouldn't it?" Jody asked.

"Huh? No, I'm not trying to think of an excuse to see him. He seems like a good kid, but my parents had him as a do-over. I'm sure he's the perfect little Japanese Baptist son they always wanted."

She wasn't sure what to make of him. On the one hand, the fact that he reached out at all should mean something, but on the other, she didn't know this kid and his motivations. Maybe he wanted her to forgive her parents so they could be a happy family again. Olivia didn't want anything to do with them. She had a cobbled together family who accepted her as she was.

"I see. So, no little puff in the Perralta-mobile?"

Olivia could tell she wanted to have some kind of probing conversation, especially with this new information. Jody's deep conversations were usually helpful and necessary, but today she simply didn't have the time.

"Sorry, I have all of these things to grade, then the interview at one. I don't know what I'm going to say even though they sent me the questions a month ago." The more she thought about the minutes ticking by and all the work she had left to do, the more she wanted to cry. Her lip began to quiver and she did her best to hide it behind one of her hands.

Not much got past Jody, who grabbed the papers and began sorting them into piles.

"What are you doing?" Olivia asked, sniffling.

"Sorting them into rough grades based on who I know and who wrote a decent introduction. We're getting this done. And then I'm going to ask you the interview questions so you sound like a decent, put-together human being on the radio." She paused for a moment and looked sharply into Olivia's eyes. "You get started reading them. Don't think too much about it, just do a skim and give a grade. Three minutes per paper."

Olivia wanted to fall to the floor and bow at Jody's feet with gratefulness. As a tear escaped her eye, she caught another pointed stare from Jody and started reading. Between the two of them, they finished the papers in record time. Olivia finally pulled up the interview questions.

Jody peeked over her shoulder. "Anything interesting in there, or just the usual?"

"The usual. What I'm working on, how it could be the biggest breakthrough in modern history." Olivia smirked. She'd done plenty of these interviews, usually after the media diluted one of her papers into pop science.

"Boring. I'll leave you to it then, cowboy."

Olivia stood and hugged her. "Thanks. You're really my favorite person." Jody winked at her and left. "One more thing left to do."

She typed out an email to Emmanuel, trying to be as brief and firm as possible. She had to have boundaries. These included not dating her exes and not engaging with a family as toxic to her as a vat of nuclear waste.

CHAPTER THIRTY-THREE

I'm fine for the millionth time, Aerin typed. While she appreciated Olivia's check-ins, she had been dozing off every time her phone buzzed with a new message. She thought about silencing the device, but if she wanted to work Olivia into a real panic, it would be by not responding at all.

Being alone in Olivia's house felt oddly intimate. Aerin could see Olivia here if she softened her gaze a little, standing in the kitchen, turning and smiling at Aerin, watching her when she wasn't looking. Olivia coming out of the shower dressed only in a towel, her short dark hair sticking up at odd angles. Olivia's absence only seemed to increase her presence in the house.

Aerin had been up most of the early morning thinking about what in the world she'd been doing on that computer. At one point, in the middle of a particularly salacious *Sunrise Lane* episode, she'd tiptoed back downstairs and tried to navigate to the site she'd been on, but it wasn't even saved in the browser history. Even if she could make it to the site, she had no clue how to access the messages. The only reason she knew there were multiple messages was because Olivia had told her. She didn't recall reading them and had only seen that last one, still on the screen in its outdated green font when she'd awakened from her trance.

Possessed by a spirit from a distant universe. It wasn't the first time she'd read that, but of course it was a ridiculous notion. How could it possibly be true? It sounded delusional, and Aerin would know. She'd heard her share of strange stories as a social worker. A man who insisted he was Mother Teresa incarnate and wanted to start a cult to facilitate other reincarnations. A young woman who was certain she'd been abducted by aliens a dozen times and had the scars to prove it. Maybe this was what it felt like to have a mental breakdown, precipitated by her divorce and realization that she was a big old lesbian. Had Pastor Ando been right all along about homosexuality?

She chuckled, amused that the thought had even crossed her mind. She knew what Pastor Ando was; she'd known for years. A monster who ruined lives to solidify his own power. A broken person trying to claw his way to heaven on the backs of his parishioners. She saw that now more than ever and felt the rage Olivia still held against him for kicking her out. It broke her heart to know she'd stood by and done nothing as it happened.

Aerin closed her eyes, eager for some real rest and the peace it normally brought. She led herself through a visualization exercise, imagining she walked along a tropical beach, a sweet-smelling breeze tickling her arms, her toes in the warm white sand. It calmed her, but the second she drifted into unconsciousness, the dream began again.

She stood at the edge of a deep canyon filled with water, a light illuminating the blue from below. Fractals of brightness danced around her and she realized she was below the surface, breathing normally and standing as though gravity pulled her the same as on land. Looking around, she saw people swimming upward, trying to reach the surface, but they were too far down, they wouldn't make it. Nothing was right about this place. How did she get here? She watched the people climb through the liquid, panic etched deeply in their faces, lips blue and lungs about to heave a mouthful of water. A few of them looked at her, trying to fathom how she could still breathe.

A few moments went by, then a deep rumble shook the water. Loose rocks fell off the cliff, floating silently into the abyss. Aerin watched the brightness grow in intensity until it blinded her and she couldn't look any longer.

By now, the low vibration reverberated through her body. The people around her scrambled, pushing one another down to save themselves. She tried to reach out and push them away, toward the surface, anything to help them outswim the light. Then the brightness turned to fire, an explosion rolling its way up through the water, blasting past Aerin and against everyone swimming. She watched them scream and fall unconscious as the fire cloud burst through with its fizzy white foam. Radioactive foam, Aerin knew as she watched her skin boil and peel off. She felt no pain as she watched the pieces of flesh float away until there were bones, then those dissolved, too. Somehow she was alive in the water without a body to hold her up.

At this moment she would awaken from the dream, her forehead sweating lightly and her hair damp against her neck. She knew those people had died, every last one of them. She couldn't dwell on the way it made her heart sink and stomach churn, though. In the back of her mind, she knew it was all her fault.

CHAPTER THIRTY-FOUR

The sun beat down on the revival tent, the hottest day of a typically sticky Indiana summer. Aerin had sweated through the back of her blue dress, and a few flyaway hairs were plastered to her cheeks. She stared at Tireville Baptist Church, looming on its tiny hill, not high by any standard, but the highest place in their flat town. Pastor Ando shot her a questioning look, an invitation to continue to set up the chairs under the revival tent. Aerin needed a break from all of this. The heat, the religion, the sloppy kisses Josh planted on her cheek. The loneliness she felt from the moment she woke up until she went to sleep. The wondering about Olivia, three long hours away.

Congregants began to arrive in their old Cadillacs and Buicks and pickup trucks. The junkier the car, the more likely the parishioner was to drive it to church, especially the maroon-colored vehicles. It was a contest of frugality. The men wore their best suits and hid their discomfort with the heat, though Aerin could see rivulets of sweat trickle down their faces.

"Aerin, are you doing God's work?" Pastor Ando shouted from the stage, where he was setting up the sound system.

Aerin, facing away, rolled her eyes and continued setting up chairs. Behind her, she heard a familiar voice talking to the pastor. Josh was congratulating him on a nice setup for the revival. What a brownnoser. She hoped he wouldn't come back to see her.

"Hey, baby," Josh said.

Her stomach dropped. Josh came up behind her and wrapped his muscled arms around her torso, planting one of his too-wet kisses on her cheek.

"Gross, Josh. And I told you to stop calling me a baby."

"Aww, you know what I mean. You're my girl and you're a babe," he said.

She shuddered. Olivia would never have called her "baby." Josh was so immature.

"He told me to help you finish up." Josh took a chair from the pile. "Here, let me get that one, too." Aerin reluctantly let him take one of the chairs in her hand. Of course she must be too delicate to put out two chairs at once. She tried not to let it bother her, to take Josh at his shallow chivalry, but it was all she could do not to scream in frustration.

Once the rows were half full, Pastor Ando started preaching. He praised the Lord for bringing everyone together to worship despite the triple digit temperatures and high humidity. Men sat with their legs wide, fanning themselves with their programs. Women were doing the same, except their legs were crossed at the ankle. If Olivia had been there, they'd have laughed at the sight of the women trying to maintain their purity in the sweltering heat.

Aerin took a seat that Josh saved her up front, only feet from Pastor Ando. She watched with a craned neck as he preached about the tortures that would befall them if they failed to adhere to the Bible's rules. It wasn't lost on her that the pastor quoted Leviticus quite a few times. She knew who he was talking to: the sinner who had committed the biggest sin of all with his daughter. She blushed as she recalled the moment before he'd walked in on them. It had been her idea to fool around in the empty church after hours on a Tuesday. She really didn't think they'd be caught, so she'd straddled Olivia on a pew, taking her shirt off as they made out. Olivia had been grabbing her ass and kissing her, hot and breathless. They were throwing their own little revival, sweaty and divine. She'd never have guessed it would be the last time she'd see Olivia.

"Aerin, he's talking to you. Stand up," Josh said impatiently.

"Huh?"

Josh rolled his eyes. "He just called you out as one of the most devoted members of the congregation."

"Oh." Aerin stood and waved to the tent behind her, then turned and nodded at the pastor. He had a gleam in his eye.

She had been an awful girlfriend, a sellout and a fraud. Religion, though, she was good at that.

Chapter Thirty-Five

Olivia absently traced her finger around the rim of a glass. The smoothness soothed her nerves as she waited for Aerin to come back from Tireville, where she'd gone for a few changes of clothes. Olivia secretly hoped she'd stay there for tonight, but she did need to observe any additional visits to mysterious websites, or other strange tunes Aerin might hum. She also needed to show her the video of the trance and see if it sent her into another one. She'd have her equipment ready this time to measure and record her brain activity.

Mr. Piddles sat on her shoulder and groomed her hair, another welcome distraction from Aerin's imminent arrival. She'd passed second-guessing the weekend-long invitation and was onto third- or fourth-guessing it. Ben's advice kept seeping into her thoughts, urging her to give Aerin another chance. She knew Aerin wanted one, which made her own reluctance more like stubbornness.

A knock on the front door drew Olivia from her thoughts. "Come in, it's open," she yelled.

Aerin stuck her head in, gave a little wave, then shut the door behind her. "I brought food. Every vegetarian dish the crappy little Chinese place in Tireville had. Sorry, it's probably cold by now."

Olivia smiled and took the bag. Aerin wasn't joking. There were at least five entrées in there and they smelled amazing. "Thanks. How much do I owe you?"

Aerin shook her head. "Oh, no, it's on me. You've donated enough of your time. The least I can do is buy dinner." She turned so they were next to each other, looking into the bag of food. Olivia blushed at the closeness and backed against the island. She slipped a twenty dollar bill from her pocket into Aerin's bag.

Aerin opened each container and removed the metal handles so they could be microwaved. Olivia watched her every move, aware that she'd pictured their life together just like this. Sharing the same space, eating meals at the same table. It was odd to be living this dream now, under such fraught circumstances. Aerin must have been thinking the same or reading her thoughts because a moment later, Olivia realized they were staring at each other. Aerin turned away first, a small smile playing at the corners of her lips, leaving Olivia with a parched throat and burning cheeks.

"Plates in here?" Aerin pointed at a cabinet. Olivia nodded, unable to find her voice.

Mr. Piddles cooed, then hopped from Olivia to Aerin's shoulder. They both froze, remembering the last time the bird had been this close to Aerin, but he didn't berate her. Instead, he nestled up to her head, as he'd done fifteen years ago in Olivia's room. Aerin looked at Olivia with eyes full of hope. Hope that Olivia felt, too, the clarity like a bucket of cold water over her head.

As Aerin turned back to find some bowls, Olivia's phone vibrated with a new message. She opened the email and drew a deep breath.

"We have it," she said quietly as she read the email.

"Hmm?" Aerin asked, the ceramic clattering against the

counter. Olivia looked up and saw Aerin staring back, wide-eyed. She'd heard.

"Look." Olivia handed her phone over with Max Pelletier's email open. He'd found the research subject from thirty years ago.

Aerin read quickly, her eyes wild with excitement. "Let's go. We have to go now." Mr. Piddles squawked and hopped into the hallway, alarmed by her change in energy.

Olivia stood to retrieve the hot food from the microwave. Frankly, all she cared about doing right now was putting some of that deliciousness into her mouth. "We can talk about this over dinner."

Aerin slammed her hand on the counter, causing Olivia's throat to hitch in surprise. "You don't understand. Whatever is in my head might seem interesting to you, but it's driving me insane. I need it out. Now." Aerin's eyes were pleading, hungry. She needed answers that Olivia couldn't give her. She needed to talk to the man in the study.

Olivia stared at her, shocked by the outburst. "Of course. I'm sorry. I'll look up flights now, but can you at least pass me a carton? I'm starving."

Aerin nodded, sliding three cartons and a fork toward her. "Thank you." Her voice was oddly calm now that Olivia had agreed.

Olivia booked them on a flight leaving for New York in just under three hours. With an hour's drive to the airport, which Olivia could take down to forty-five minutes, they'd have just enough time to pack and stuff the rest of the food into their mouths.

Mr. Piddles did not like the news that he'd be alone for a few days, but Olivia left out plenty of food and water, plus some extra treats. She texted Jody to come check in on him, and didn't wait for a response. Jody would do anything for the bird she called her godson. Once Olivia packed clothes for herself and Aerin into a backpack, they were off.

The plane ride started off smoothly, a relief to Olivia, who'd forgotten to take a Dramamine. She couldn't remember the last time she'd flown without one and she prayed it wouldn't be a disaster. Luckily, she'd remembered headphones, so she watched reruns of *Sunrise Lane* on the Soap Opera Channel. Aerin stared out the window at the part of the sunset only visible above the clouds, transfixed by the oranges and pinks against the thick wisps. Olivia had started to fall asleep, her head resting against the back of her seat, when she felt the first drop.

She jerked to attention, gripping the seat's arms and shutting her eyes against the turbulence. Another drop, then some nauseating jerking as the captain came on the loudspeaker. Just some turbulence, he said. Nothing to be worried about. Olivia's stomach churned and she began to regret the Chinese food. Just as she knew she would throw up any second, she felt a warm hand gently pry hers off the arm. Aerin slipped her fingers between Olivia's, projecting an immediate calmness through her body. Olivia felt the softness of Aerin's skin against hers, felt Aerin inside her mind telling her that nothing bad would happen if she gave in. Just let go, she seemed to say.

Somehow it worked. The adrenaline stopped pumping through her body and her damp forehead began to dry. Olivia closed her eyes and imagined she was Mr. Piddles, thrilled to be coasting at thirty thousand feet, the wind under her feathers, lifting and dropping her gently. She soared in her mind until another violent bout of turbulence shook the plane. She gripped Aerin's hand, felt it lift, and inhaled sharply as her knuckles touched Aerin's lips. A jolt of pleasure traveled from her hand to her stomach, tingling all the nerves along the way.

She shivered. The brief kiss ended quickly, and Olivia looked up to see Aerin looking intensely uncomfortable.

"I'm sorry. I wasn't thinking," she whispered. Aerin let go of her hand. Olivia wished she'd stop thinking again, a message Aerin must have received but didn't act upon. Olivia intertwined their fingers, pulling their hands to her lap. If there was any chance of this plane going down, she wanted this to be her final memory.

CHAPTER THIRTY-SIX

Tireville High's annual mid-April field trip was a day at the Indianapolis Science Museum. On the bus ride home, Olivia and Aerin sat next to each other in silence. They'd exhausted all their energy walking through exhibits on Newtonian physics, electricity, and a special gallery of medical anomalies. Most of the boys in their class spent as much time as possible there, looking at the wall of brains in jars, the deformed fetuses, and an interactive giant heart attack sculpture. Olivia and Aerin had been transfixed by the jars, standing close enough to one another to accidentally brush hands every once in a while.

"What do you think these people were like?" Aerin had asked.

Olivia shrugged. "I think most of them were babies, so I guess like nothing. This one is a man in his fifties." She pointed to a larger brain in a bigger jar, submerged in formaldehyde. "Maybe he was a good person, like a teacher or something."

"Being a teacher doesn't make you a good person."

Olivia turned to Aerin, a dreamy look in her eyes. "You're so smart. And you're right. I guess I mean that maybe he tried to do good things in life."

"And then maybe at the end, he secretly murdered his wife and buried her body in their yard. And then he was so distraught, he hung himself," Aerin said. She felt Olivia take her hand and squeeze it.

"Gross. But yeah, maybe." They'd smiled at each other.

On the bus, their eyes met in silent conversation. Olivia's hand brushed the back of Aerin's and sent shivers down her spine. It felt deliciously illicit, surrounded by classmates who didn't know the two were deeply in love. So deeply they'd vowed to marry each other someday if it became legal.

The two kids across the aisle were engrossed in a Game Boy and everyone else had either dozed off or was staring out the window. Aerin didn't need the distraction of electronics or the passing cornfields. She could look into Olivia's eyes forever. They were brown, with flecks of gold that glistened in bright sunlight. She and Olivia seemed to have a whole conversation between themselves, silently, through an upturn of Olivia's mouth or a narrowing of Aerin's eyes. Olivia's lips curled into a smile and Aerin bit her lip, trying to keep her thoughts tame when she wanted nothing more than to kiss that smile away, turn it into heavy breathing and sweat and sweetness. She knew what those lips could do and she had a feeling there was even more to explore in that arena.

Olivia seemed to understand Aerin's fixation on her mouth, so she wet her lips and shifted slightly so the back of her head was against the bus window. The green vinyl of the seat and the rubbery, sickly smell of the school bus did nothing to stop them both from imagining what they could be doing in Aerin's bed. Olivia smiled again and adjusted the sleeves of her white T-shirt, bringing her hand down over Aerin's, entwining their fingers. The way Olivia looked at her, the feeling of her thumb brushing the back of Aerin's, made her underwear warm and slippery.

"You're coming over?" Aerin mouthed into the rattling of the bus.

Olivia's eyes darkened as she nodded and Aerin's heart swelled with desire. She couldn't wait until they were old enough to spend as much time as they wanted together, away from Tireville and its prying eyes.

CHAPTER THIRTY-SEVEN

The airport stank of exhaust fumes that made Olivia's residual nausea even worse. She and Aerin made quite a pair, each in their own personal hell, making their way to Ground Transportation. She wanted to retch and Aerin flinched as each new voice or sound entered the cacophony of echoing shouts and rolling luggage. Olivia could see how each new sound cracked Aerin open, slowly leaving her shell-less, exposed. After what had happened on the plane, she felt a new closeness with Aerin. They were a team, not researcher and research subject. A team that had to get the hell out of the airport.

After they'd climbed into a taxi, Olivia gave the driver Murray Sandelman's address. As she did, she had a sudden realization, as if she'd just awakened from a hazy dream.

"Aerin, it's almost eleven. We can't show up at someone's house right now." She waited for a moment. She expected Aerin to disagree, to insist on the normalcy, or necessity, of going to a stranger's house at midnight to inquire about something that happened decades ago.

"Okay, let's get a hotel."

Olivia raised her eyebrows. "Really?"

"Yeah, you seem tired," Aerin said.

Olivia watched the streetlights flash across Aerin's face as they drove out of the terminal, expecting to see some of the urgency from earlier in the evening. "Okay. Can you take us to a hotel?" she asked the driver. He looked in the rearview mirror and nodded. "A decent one, if you can."

"Okay, no problem. We go to the Holiday Inn?" he asked in a thick Eastern European accent.

"Sounds good," she said, and the driver slowed to take the exit back toward the airport.

Olivia turned to smile at Aerin, but she was staring out the window, entranced by the planes landing and taking off again. Olivia sighed. It would be nice to have the old Aerin back, the one who didn't disappear into a fragment of herself every few hours. The one she'd fallen in love with, who she could imagine loving again.

At the hotel, she left Aerin by the fireplace as she checked them in.

"You really don't have any double rooms left?" she asked the front desk clerk. She leaned heavily on her elbows as she took in the scene in the lobby. Lots of parents wearing youth baseball jerseys in various states of drunkenness milled about, chatting with each other.

"I'm sorry, ma'am, we only have two rooms that aren't booked. You can see that we're a little busy. The Little League World Series is in town. Would you like the accessible room with a queen bed, or the king?" The woman clearly wasn't interested in Olivia's whining, so she relented and asked for the king room. At least they wouldn't be sleeping on top of one another.

Key cards in hand, she went back to fetch Aerin so they could turn in. She needed a comfortable pillow on a soft mattress right now like she needed oxygen. Olivia sucked in a breath and did a double take as she looked around the lobby, glancing past the unlit fireplace and breakfast nook. She could have sworn she'd left Aerin at the chairs, but the only people sitting there were baseball dads. Had she been mistaken? Or had Aerin simply walked away?

She broke out into a cold sweat, panicking like a mother who'd just lost her child. Spinning slowly, she reached as far into each corner as she could with her gaze. Just a smattering of parents on their second winds. She felt herself going crazy imagining that Aerin had just left the hotel, maybe caught a cab into Forest Hills, or maybe a plane to somewhere else on a whim. Olivia's throat constricted and the lobby closed in on her. She couldn't lose Aerin again, not in a big, unfamiliar city.

Then she heard something, a familiar laugh in the distance. She followed it around a corner and into the hotel restaurant, empty save for Aerin at the bar, flirting with the bartender as he passed her a drink. The lights were dim and the place looked half-shuttered.

Olivia's panic quickly faded and a flash of anger rose in its place. Not only had Aerin wandered off without telling her, she was making new friends, maybe to get free drinks, maybe for fun. Olivia just wanted to go to bed, not deal with an ex who might be trying to hook up with someone else.

"Aerin," she said. She wanted to admonish her for walking away, for making Olivia think that she'd left her again, but the words didn't come.

"Hey, I got thirsty. Do you want something?" Aerin asked simply like Olivia's ears weren't ringing with rage.

She seethed. "No. I'm going to bed. Here's your key." The second room key clattered as she threw it on the counter. "Room 419."

She turned on her heel and walked out of the restaurant, through the hallway, and up the fire stairs. When she got to the room, she threw her backpack on the chair and plunged facedown onto the bed, letting silent tears stream down her face. She didn't have any right to be upset about Aerin's behavior with the bartender, but the flirting bothered her. Maybe Aerin just wasn't as interested in her as she'd thought. Through the lens of exhaustion, Aerin's behavior seemed like a personal betrayal. After all, she'd dropped everything, bought tickets for them both, and Aerin just walked away without telling her? She sighed into her pillow. At least they could comfortably slip back into a purely working relationship with no hint of intimacy.

Olivia fell asleep eventually, after she'd stopped soaking her pillow with jealous tears. At some point she dreamed Aerin came into bed and spooned her, her arm gently resting on Olivia's middle. She felt the most comfortable she'd been in a long time, even if it was just a dream.

Olivia woke up at half past eight the next morning, yawning deeply after a restful night. She listened for Aerin in the bathroom; perhaps she had gone in and not yet come out. After a long while, Olivia determined that the only sound was the toilet flushing next door. Had Aerin come up to the room at all?

She got up to use the bathroom and caught a hint of burnt sugar. Aerin's lotion, it had to be. She'd been here. As she plodded toward the toilet, Olivia noticed a note on the bathroom vanity. She squeezed her eyes shut to clear them of their haziness and read it while she peed. At least Aerin had the decency to give her a heads-up this time. She quickly brushed her teeth and threw on a new set of clothes, then headed downstairs to catch the first cab she could find.

She had no idea how long Aerin had been alone at Murray's apartment.

CHAPTER THIRTY-EIGHT

"Can't you go any faster? We just missed the light." Olivia groaned, failing miserably at hiding her frustration.

The taxi driver just shook his head and glared at her in the rearview mirror. Olivia crossed her arms and stared out the window, lips pursed. She was acting childish but she was scared for Aerin and, if she was honest, scared of Aerin too. Something had shifted once they got on that plane to New York. Aerin seemed to become bolder, reckless, closer to her carefree, risk-taking kid self at twelve than the mature adult she should be. Not that Olivia would necessarily mind in better circumstances.

When the driver stopped short in front of the address, Olivia gave him a large tip to make up for her crabbiness. He nodded gruffly and sped off. A row of large apartment buildings crowded the skyline across the street. She spotted Murray's address in the center, a yellowish brick building that had grayed in the city air. Across the street she ascended the concrete stairs to the entrance. Behind her, cars honked at each other and a driver yelled at a pedestrian for crossing too slowly. She buzzed with anxiety and discomfort. This city, more claustrophobic and angry than Chicago, was not for her.

A small fountain fizzled in the courtyard, a sculpture of

two swans intertwined at the neck with bright red tulips all around. The breeze should have smelled fresh and summery but instead carried a hint of sewage and rankness. She welcomed the air-conditioning and commercial cleaner smell of the lobby. A doorman named Reggie welcomed her.

"Are you here to see someone?" he asked.

"Yeah, Murray Sandelman?"

"You're in the right place. Do you want me to give him a call, or is he expecting you?" The doorman retreated behind his desk and picked up the phone, poised to dial.

Murray might not be expecting me, but Aerin sure as hell should be, she thought. "Oh, no, he's expecting me. Actually, do you recall seeing a woman in her early thirties come through here this morning? Long brown hair? Also here to see Murray?"

The doorman set the phone down and looked at her strangely. "I came in at six this morning and the guy who does the overnight, Larry, mentioned someone who came in about four. He said she was the nicest girl, but real strange. So, when I get in, he tells me about this girl and he shows me the security tape. They never speak," he said.

"Huh?"

"He talks to everyone, especially in the middle of the night because you can get a little bored here, but this girl—"

"Woman," Olivia interjected.

"Yeah, anyway, she comes in at four a.m. and just stares at Larry, smiles at him, and he smiles back at her. Then she nods and so does he. It's like they had a whole conversation in their heads. Weirdest thing, Larry doesn't remember any of it, only that he thought she was nice. He honestly thought they'd had a whole conversation out loud, like he does with everyone."

Olivia took a deep breath. "Yeah, that was her. She's been here this whole time?"

"Haven't seen her leave. Unless she's got other superpowers and flew out the window or something," Reggie said.

"Who knows," Olivia muttered. At this point, nothing would surprise her. "Thanks for your help, Reggie. I should head up." Reggie tipped his hat at her and returned to his post by the door.

The elevator glistened in ornate gold with blue fringes, a relic from the twenties. Olivia prayed it wouldn't break down on its slow journey to the seventh floor. She tapped her foot impatiently as it chimed to announce it had reached its destination, then took its time opening up. Finally, she made it to Murray's apartment door. As soon as she raised her hand to knock, Aerin opened it. Olivia sucked in her breath and tried to remember how angry she was at this woman. To her credit, Aerin did look a bit sheepish at the sight of Olivia, like she knew she'd behaved badly but couldn't stop herself.

Olivia raised her eyebrows and crossed her arms. "I know you're an adult, but we came here together and I don't appreciate you abandoning me in the hotel. Twice," she said, holding up two fingers.

Aerin nodded. "I know. I'm sorry about that. You seemed tired, so I wanted to let you sleep. I hope you did sleep well," she said. Something hid behind her words.

Had she actually dreamt that Aerin had held her? She looked at Aerin curiously and decided not to read into any implications. "Where's Murray?"

"This way," Aerin said. They walked down a small hallway, its walls covered in drawings of strange landscapes and machines surrounded by mathematical equations. A small stack of books on extraterrestrial life sat neatly against the doorjamb. As she approached what looked like a small, outdated kitchen, a faint electric hum set her neck hair on end. Olivia looked down at her arm. It had goose bumps and the hair was standing straight up as if she were touching an electric fence.

Aerin turned back at the same instant Olivia crumpled to the floor.

CHAPTER THIRTY-NINE

Olivia's head swirled as she started to come to. She heard voices in the background, distant, spiraling together, then unwinding.

"I don't know what happened. She just fell," said a woman close to her face. Aerin?

"We're more powerful together than I thought," a man with a heavy New York accent said.

Olivia stirred, groaning at the light filtering into the room. When she finally blinked her eyes open, she found Aerin and Murray staring down at her.

"What happened?" She tried to lift her head and an ache shot through her neck. "Ow."

A moment of silence passed. "Are you telling me I can fix this?" Aerin asked.

Olivia almost responded before she realized Aerin's question had been directed at Murray, who stared into Aerin's eyes and nodded every few seconds. They seemed to be having a silent conversation.

Olivia scrunched her eyebrows. "What the—"

Aerin turned to her, completely serene. "You're going to be fine. You fainted and we brought you to the couch. Let me just sit over here so you can put your head on my lap," she said.

While it was the last place Olivia wanted to put her head at the moment, she felt compelled to do it anyway. Aerin tentatively placed her fingers at Olivia's collarbone, tracing the ridges tenderly. She felt instantly buoyant, like they were playing a magical adult version of a game they frequently played as children: light as a feather, stiff as a board. Her heart began to race as Aerin slipped a hand down the back of her shirt, massaging her shoulders. All of the anger and confusion she'd felt toward Aerin since they arrived in the city lifted away like a cloud. She imagined Aerin's hands everywhere, touching every inch of her skin, massaging, kneading. She'd almost let out an involuntary moan when Aerin's hands suddenly stilled.

"You're healed," Aerin said. Olivia looked up at her, biting her bottom lip. Aerin's cheeks were flushed and her eyes were everywhere but on Olivia. I want you so much right now, Olivia thought. *Me too*, came a distant response.

"Let's get her sitting up," Murray said, gesturing toward one end of the couch.

Aerin gently lifted Olivia's head off her lap and nudged her to sit. Olivia tested her neck, rolling it from side to side without any discomfort. In fact, she felt looser than she did on a normal day.

The couch springs groaned as she positioned herself to face Aerin. "How did you do that?"

Aerin thought for a moment, wringing her hands together. "It wasn't me. It's, um, well, I can't pronounce its name in English, but it's the thing that's inside me. Murray told me everything."

Olivia stared at Murray, who sat on the coffee table. His veins were blue against paper-thin skin. He had to be at least ninety. White stubble dotted the crevices of his wrinkled cheeks and his hair was a thin array of wiry white sprouts protruding in all directions from his scalp.

"Come with me, both of you," he said. Slowly, he pushed himself up from the table and hobbled to the kitchen. "See? No cane anymore," he said to Aerin, and she chuckled. Well, weren't they just the best of friends.

Olivia steadied herself on Aerin's shoulder as they followed him. "He's talking about how he's feeling much better since I arrived in the city," Aerin said. Olivia didn't understand. Did this have to do with the reason she fainted? "You can ask him anything once we sit down, but you'll have to hurry. We need your help."

She nodded, confused, still trying to shake off the fogginess from passing out. So far, this trip had not exactly gone according to plan.

"Sit, sit." Murray pointed to one of three chairs around a fake marble table. He wore a ratty gray jogging suit opened to a stained tank top underneath. A pile of dirty dishes teetered out of the sink and onto the counter. "Have some bread." He placed half a loaf of stale challah and some honey in front of her. "You need to eat."

Olivia nodded, tearing off a small piece of the bread and dipping it into the honey. She let it melt in her mouth. Somehow, despite the dry sponginess of the bread, it tasted sweeter than anything she could remember.

"Good, right?" Murray asked. She nodded and he winked at her. "So, your questions. Let's talk."

Olivia swallowed her mouthful. "Okay. Why did I pass out?"

Murray chuckled. "Well, that's kind of a boring one to start out with, don't you think?"

Olivia scoffed. "No. I walked in here, I passed out. That's not normal, and I would know. I'm an expert. What the hell happened?"

He nodded in Aerin's direction and she spoke. "Murray and I have alien energy in our bodies. Extraterrestrial. Whatever you want to call it. It's not from our universe. Anyway, I'm not used to controlling it yet, so I let a little too much of my energy mix with Murray's and it overwhelmed your brain, like an electric current through the air. I'm sorry."

"Sure, okay. Let's say I buy your theory. Why, then? How did they get here? Why are you both possessed by aliens? Why you two specifically?" Why Aerin? The thought struck her hard and she took a deep breath. Her Aerin, the one she'd loved, had been replaced by an unpredictable person who could read her mind and was prone to wild behavioral swings. She hadn't realized that alongside her conflicted feelings about having Aerin back, she mourned the person she had been. The people they'd both been.

"How do you get it out?" Olivia asked meekly, exhausted by her own stream of consciousness. "How does Aerin go back to being the person she was?"

"Ah, now you're talking," said Murray.

"So?" Olivia asked.

"We don't know. That's why we need your help. Something brought us together. I've been in pretty bad shape lately, but the moment you two flew into the city, I've felt better. I don't know why, but I think the alien in me is waking up. It's starting to get energized. After thirty years, it had about given up. It's getting ready for something. I think it was just waiting for Aerin to come along." He shrugged his bony shoulders.

Aerin shifted in her seat and reached for the loaf of bread. "I forgot how hungry I was," she said, shoving a piece into her mouth. "Murray thinks there's a huge communication barrier between us and them, so they have to send us messages in roundabout ways."

"Music," Olivia said.

Murray nodded. "Yes, and visions and dreams. And you're the key to getting them translated for us so we can understand. It's like if you have a Jew from the old country talking to an Ethiopian Jew, they need the translator. That's you."

Olivia caught on, albeit cautiously. "So you're the old country Jews and the alien, or whatever you think it is, is the Ethiopian Jew?" She should have come up with a less awkward metaphor before repeating it back.

Aerin nodded. "Yeah. Basically that's right."

Okay. Olivia would go with this theory for now. There didn't seem to be a better one. "What are they trying to tell you?"

Murray and Aerin exchanged glances. "Remember my dream? The one about the bomb?" Aerin asked.

"When you woke up in the basement on that internet forum thing?"

"Yeah. Well, I have the same dream every time I go to sleep. A bomb goes off underwater and people drown. Murray can't tell for sure, but it seems like we're supposed to stop it. That's how I always feel at the end of the dream, like I could have stopped it and saved everyone."

Olivia scoffed. "I'm sorry, what? You're supposed to stop a bomb? How exactly do you plan to do that?"

Murray answered. "We're not sure yet. We were hoping you could help us find out. We need you to run some EEGs on us and send it to your friend."

"Stanton. He knew how to translate them," Aerin said.

"But I don't have any equipment with me. I'll have to go back to Indiana."

"No time," Aerin and Murray said in unison.

Aerin squeezed Olivia's forearm. "I know you won't want to do this, but we can borrow some equipment from the hospital up the street."

"They won't let me borrow—oh." Olivia said, suddenly understanding. They were stealing. Okay, this was too far. She was about to protest when she felt a very marked intrusion in her mind. She turned to Aerin slowly, unsure of what she'd find in her eyes. She saw extreme concentration. "Did you just censor my thoughts?"

"Well, yeah," Aerin said as if it were the most natural thing in the world. "We have to do this. People's lives depend on you getting the machine."

Olivia felt her stomach drop. She stood and glared at Aerin. "What else have you been planting in my head?"

Aerin knitted her eyebrows together and shook her head. "I don't know what you mean. I haven't—"

"Really?" Olivia crossed her arms and stared hard into Aerin's eyes. "Because there are a lot of things I've been thinking about and doing that seem pretty out of character for me."

Aerin looked at Murray and then back up. "I—if it happened, it wasn't intentional. Please. We need you." Aerin tried to put a hand on her arm, but she pulled away quickly.

"I can't be here," Olivia said. Everything that had happened between them, the desire, the looks, it had been a lie. Aerin had made her fall in love all over again to secure her position as an accomplice in all this madness. "No, I can't be here anymore. Don't try to stop me." She looked pointedly at Aerin.

Olivia rushed out the door without a second thought, skipped the elevator, and took flight after flight of stairs down to the lobby. Reggie nodded at her as she sprinted past, through the glass doors, and into the bright daylight. She chose a direction and began to jog, not caring where she ended up. She only cared that it was as far from Aerin and Murray as possible.

CHAPTER FORTY

Olivia stared blankly at a family of ducks swimming up a stream in Central Park. This area of the park was relatively quiet, as far as New York went. She needed time to contemplate her next move. None of the options seemed like good ones. For one, she could fly back to Indiana, leaving Aerin stranded in New York with a stranger, although they did seem to be getting along just fine. Or she could return to Murray's and submit herself to the mind control of one person she hardly knew and another she wasn't sure she did.

The best choice was to catch a plane, go home, and leave this all behind her. Not think about Aerin like they'd ever had another chance, not get involved in some ridiculous conspiracy theory involving aliens. She was 98 percent sure she wanted to choose Option A. But the 2 percent of her that considered Option B left too much reasonable doubt. If she didn't help Aerin and Murray, a bomb went off, and a lot of people died, how could she live with herself? They were calling her bluff. Aerin had let her leave the apartment because she knew Olivia couldn't refuse. At most, if she went back to Murray's, she'd only be putting herself in danger. Maybe that was a price she had to pay.

Olivia squeezed her hands into fists and groaned. A German shepard walking by with its owner whimpered and moved to the other side of the path.

"You okay?" the owner asked. He looked nice enough, but Olivia really didn't need strangers inquiring about her problems right now.

"Yeah, fine." She pushed off the bench and walked in the other direction. The wind picked up and dried the sweat that had begun to moisten her forehead as she made her way back into the city. She walked without thought, stopping only to purchase a bottle of water and a falafel from a street vendor. Eventually, she realized she needed to figure out where the heck she'd traveled. In front of her was a sign to the Queensboro Bridge. A direct path back to Forest Hills, according to her phone. Olivia sighed and threw her hands up. She felt like screaming in defiance of her situation; how else should she act when her entire newly formed friendship with her ex-girlfriend turned out to be a giant farce?

The late afternoon sun began to weigh against the buildings, forcing shadows to bend into the streets. According to her phone, Murray's apartment was still a couple hours away on foot. Good, Olivia thought. They can wait. She would take her time getting back, make them worry about her.

An hour later, Olivia began to rethink her plan to walk all the way to Forest Hills. She wanted to drag this out as long as possible, like a teenager, slamming the door just a few more times to really make a point. She stopped at a bar for a drink and a sandwich. As she sat at a high top cradling a gin and tonic, Olivia recalled all of the odd objects in Murray's apartment. The drawings, the books, the equations, they all seemed to indicate either that he was a few crayons short of a full box or that he had gained some kind of deep understanding of whatever had happened to both him and Aerin. She wondered if he'd ever been like Aerin, frightened and unaware, secretly influencing other people.

She pulled up the email Max had sent, looking for a phone number buried in his long signature. Male academics were notorious for sharing every tiny accolade they'd earned during their entire educations and careers, including distinctions that mattered to nobody. She dialed the number, hoping he had nothing better to do on a weekend night than hang out by his phone. One ring. Two. Five. As she'd about given up, she heard a voice on the other end.

"Sorry, hang on," Max said in a heavy French accent to someone in the background. "Hello?" he said to Olivia.

She hesitated for a moment. "Uh, hi. Max Pelletier? This is Dr. Olivia Ando from the University of Indiana."

"Oh, oh, yes, Dr. Ando. I see you received my message. How can I help you?"

Olivia shifted in her seat. She wasn't sure, but she might as well start somewhere. "I met Murray today. I have some questions."

"Ah, yes. How does he look?"

"Actually, pretty good for his age. Off the record, it seems like just being around my friend—er, my research subject, has enhanced his own well-being. Or so he says." Max let out a harsh breath that Olivia couldn't read and she continued. "Listen, I need some information. I found out today that my research subject has been influencing my thoughts. I wondered if you had the same experience with Murray."

Max didn't speak for a long moment. Olivia thought he'd hung up when he cleared his throat. "Yes, I have often wondered that myself. Murray came to me in a bit of a strange way. I'm not sure how he found me. I was not doing this kind of research at the time. I'm almost positive that I did not choose to write the paper of my own free will. The content, maybe that was mine, but not the idea for it."

Olivia let that sink in. "What do you mean?" she asked.

"I was hoping you'd uncover something that would help explain it to me."

She hadn't uncovered much of anything at all. "What were you doing around the time you met Murray?"

"I had a band and we toured all over Europe and Canada. I met Murray after one of my shows. He said he had followed me on tour for three weeks. I was also working as a hypnotist. I did past life regressions mainly and I knew it wasn't real, but they thought it was, so that's how I paid my bills," he said.

Olivia rolled her eyes. She couldn't believe people believed that past life crap. "Okay. Just out of curiosity, what kind of music did your band play?"

"Oh, we were a very well-regarded jazz band at the time. We mostly played Third Stream," he said.

Olivia's breath caught in her throat. Jazz music? That seemed like a strange coincidence. "What was your band called?"

"We were the Fifth Harmonics. Murray came up to me one night after a show and said my music spoke to him. The next thing I knew, I was getting my PhD in neurology and publishing this paper. Murray was in and out of my life then, but I had all the notes from our time together."

"Very strange," Olivia said. She let the information roll around in her mind for a moment. "I have one more thing to ask you. Do you recall sending messages back and forth with a Hans Schilling in the early eighties?"

This time, Max's gasp made more sense. "Well, yes, in a private forum. How did you hear about this?"

"Aer—I mean, my research subject found it. She logged on to some kind of forum one night. I saw her do it. She wasn't entirely conscious."

"No, that makes no sense. I am sure it no longer exists. It was my family's bulletin board system, and then I invited some close friends to use it. Hans was a friend of the family's and we kept a correspondence for years. My father kept the BBS running until the early nineties when we switched to email. I'm positive it is no longer online."

Olivia felt a knot forming in her throat. None of this made any sense. "I have screenshots. Do you want me to send them?"

"Please do. Listen, I don't think I can help you anymore right now. I'll be in touch." His breath sounded ragged.

Olivia started to say good-bye, but the call had already dropped. She leaned her head against her fists and stared at her half empty drink. On a whim, she searched for the Fifth Harmonics. She came across a poorly scanned newspaper article from the late seventies with a pixelated photograph of the band performing in Calgary. She scanned the names under the photo. Max was listed as the bassist and vocalist. The other names she didn't recognize, but as she examined the picture, her heart stopped. A man who looked exactly like Stanton Carlile Jones III peeked over Max's shoulder. Just visible in his hands was an alto saxophone.

CHAPTER FORTY-ONE

The photograph chilled Olivia, even though she told herself it had to be a coincidence. Lots of saxophone players probably looked like Stanton, especially in a badly digitized newspaper article. She knew the "all Asians look the same" trope and she was applying the same stereotype with Stanton. No, this had to be a different dark-skinned guy with that same expression Stanton always had, like he was listening to you, but also light-years away. It had to be. Stanton was what, thirty years old? This guy looked about thirty. Therefore, they could not possibly be the same person, she told herself. Something about it still felt off.

She needed to get back to Murray's now that she understood Aerin's desperate need for answers, now that she sought her own. A cab whisked her straight to his apartment where she ran up the steps and into the lobby.

Reggie had been replaced by a younger man who nodded at her as she passed. Her legs ached from walking so she took the elevator, which seemed even slower this time. She approached Murray's door and walked right in. Both of them would know it was her just by thinking, or whatever they did.

Indeed, they sat comfortably on the couch as she stepped

into the dimly lit room. "Don't you want to turn on some lights?"

"Go for it. Welcome back," Aerin said. She got up from the couch and walked toward Olivia, hesitating a moment before embracing her. Olivia felt warm and energized. She leaned into the hug against her better judgment.

"Can we talk? I want to apologize," Aerin said.

She spoke so tenderly that Olivia had no trouble agreeing. "Okay." She followed Aerin into the kitchen.

"I'll understand if you don't believe me, but I never intentionally put thoughts into your head, except the one time this morning."

Olivia nodded, scanning Aerin's eyes for the truth. She seemed to be telling it. A clock tick-tocked in the background as she thought for a moment. "Honestly, I don't know if it matters anymore. We should probably focus on what you need to do to save those people."

Aerin's eyes lit up and she clasped her hands together. "Really? You'll help?"

"I don't think I have a choice," she said.

"Thank you, thank you, thank you." Aerin squeezed Olivia's fingers. "While you were gone, Murray and I came up with a plan to get an EEG machine. Murray can relay it all to you so you'll know exactly what's going to happen."

"What if I hadn't come back?" Olivia asked, suddenly aware that they were completely unperturbed that she'd been out for hours.

"Oh, well you were going to. Come back, that is. Sorry, this is probably another weird thing I should have told you earlier."

Olivia crossed her arms and sat in one of the old kitchen chairs. "What, exactly?"

"Well, Murray and I can see the future, just a little bit. We knew you'd come back tonight."

"Just a little bit? Jesus, I don't even want to know. Never mind. Let's just get this over with." Olivia shook her head.

CHAPTER FORTY-TWO

Aerin joined hands with Murray, giving him extra energy to impart the plan on to Olivia through mind visualization. He probably didn't need the extra contact with Aerin in such close proximity, but she knew her participation put Olivia at ease.

She watched Murray think through the mission, floating through a back door of the hospital as if he were a ghost. He clearly hadn't ever seen the back of this particular hospital; it looked a little too much like Seattle Grace. She thought she saw Dr. Grey back there smoking a cigarette. Did she even smoke? Once they were through the wall, they wandered through the corridors until they came to an elevator. This part was clearer. Murray had been in that elevator and remembered its blue floor and silver walls. They got off at one of the floors—the number wasn't visible—and found a neat stack of EEG machines. Aerin didn't think that was what they would look like, but she wasn't the expert. She also doubted they'd be so accessible.

Sure, the entire plan was vaguer than she'd like, but at least they had one. And having a plan was better than not having a plan. They just needed Olivia's buy-in. Once they got to the hospital, Murray would corrupt the security camera footage and they'd figure out the rest.

"Do you see?" Aerin asked. She already knew the answer, but Olivia would want to feel like she had some say in this, even though it frustrated Aerin to have to play along. If Olivia experienced the carnage she saw every time she fell asleep, she couldn't possibly refuse to help. Had she not already agreed on her own, Aerin might have tried more subtle manipulation.

Olivia nodded, her golden brown eyes flicking briefly to meet Aerin's. They were still as captivating as ever, maybe more so after their argument earlier. A fire flared behind them that Aerin had never forgotten, the passion that drew them together in the first place. Her skin prickled with pleasure the same way it had when she'd healed Olivia. Huh. This feeling was new, intense and intoxicating.

"I have some uniforms in my closet," Murray said. Olivia raised her eyebrows. "Don't ask. Things I've picked up over the years."

Aerin shrugged. "Good. I guess I'll take a nurse's uniform if you have one, and Olivia should put on a lab coat." She felt her heartbeat pick up as she imagined what Olivia would look like in one of those.

"Too bad you didn't tell me about this earlier. I have one with my name and everything back home," Olivia said bitterly. So, not totally on board yet, but getting there. Maybe she'd give her a little nudge in the right direction.

CHAPTER FORTY-THREE

They arrived at Queens Memorial Hospital around midnight. Murray had the taxi driver drop them at the ER, which was quietly busy at this hour. The three of them discreetly assumed their roles. Aerin was wearing scrubs with an old sweatshirt of Murray's to cover the top. She took off the sweatshirt and caught a glimpse of herself in a window. She smiled. She looked exactly like her mom.

Olivia didn't have to try very hard to carry herself with the air of a doctor. She wore the white coat with a confidence that kept Aerin on edge, aware of each movement Olivia made, each tiny thought that went through her mind. How she could be so attracted to someone who, on the surface, was wildly off-limits mystified her. But that was a conundrum for later.

They silently communicated part one of their plan. Olivia walked around the back. Aerin found a wheelchair that had been left on the curb and brought it to Murray, who pretended to be less mobile than he was. Not difficult for a man who, two days ago, could barely balance with a cane. If all went well, the three of them would meet in the middle of the hospital near the elevators.

The main doors opened for Aerin and the sharp sanitary

smell hit her right away. They made their way past the emergency room, through a brightly lit linoleum hallway, and into an adjacent corridor, empty save for a couple of hospital beds lining the walls. Up ahead she saw a sign pointing to the central elevators, which they'd take up to some yet-to-be-determined floor. Hopefully that was where they'd find an EEG to steal. She'd only seen the two that Olivia had used on her, so it would be up to Olivia to figure out what they needed.

She heard footsteps around the corner and held her breath as they approached. An audible sigh escaped her lips as Olivia appeared. "Hi," Aerin said.

"Are we ready? Once we get to the neurology department, I can take a guess about where the machines are stored," Olivia whispered loudly. She jerked her head toward the elevators. "Follow me."

Aerin rolled Murray at a brisk pace to keep up with Olivia, who speed-walked to the elevators. Just as they arrived, the doors opened. All three of them froze as a man in his thirties emerged from the car, passing them a distracted nod. Olivia nodded back collegially. Aerin smiled to herself. She loved Olivia's confidence.

"Neurology, third floor." Olivia pressed the button.

"Got to give it to you, ladies. Really pulling off the looks," Murray said with a gleam in his eye.

Aerin smacked him gently on the head. "Stop it, you dirty old man." To her relief, Olivia laughed. And laughed and laughed.

"What the fuck are we doing?" She put her hands on her knees. "I can't fucking believe this. Who would have thought I would be here right now trying to steal a fucking machine from a fucking hospital?" Tears rolled down her face and Aerin concentrated hard on sobering her up.

Just as the elevator dinged and the doors started to open, Aerin jammed them shut again. Olivia turned to her, wiping her face. "What are you doing? We're here."

"You're overtired. You need to get a grip before we go out there. Come on. Game face." She put her hands on Olivia's cheeks, wiping the remaining tears away and forcing Olivia to look at her. "In and out of here, okay?"

Olivia nodded, her expression turning serious. She shook out her arms and opened the elevator doors, striding forward without a glance back at Aerin and Murray. She walked slowly, but not too slowly. It was the walk of someone who knew where they were going. She walked past rooms with numbers, some with signs. Most of them were dark, but there were a few patients here being treated. She pointed discreetly to a small sign that read "Supplies." Aerin parked the wheelchair outside the door, mentally reminding Murray to be the lookout.

Olivia cursed under her breath. "So stupid. Door's locked. We need an ID."

Aerin looked at it for a moment. "I don't know. I think I might be able to open it." She put her hand on the card reader and concentrated all of her energy into it. She wasn't sure exactly what kind of energy she needed to apply or how much, so she just went for it. A moment later, the blinking red light turned green. Olivia looked at her with wonder and she shrugged, feeling warm with the attention.

The small room held shelves of neatly packed machines and test supplies. Olivia found the equipment quickly, a plastic rectangle with slots for wires. She grabbed a roll of medical tape and lifted her shirt. "Here, you have to attach it. I'm not walking out of here with one of these in my hand."

Aerin looked Olivia in the eye before her gaze fell to the exposed skin. Her throat went dry and she tried to clear it, to no avail. She was somehow supposed to concentrate on their plan while she touched Olivia's skin, albeit for the benefit of said plan? "Yeah, uh, I'll get it."

Olivia tore piece after piece of tape off with her teeth and handed them to Aerin, who affixed the machine to Olivia's lower right abdomen. Every time her fingers touched Olivia, she shuddered a little. Being around Murray and all his energy seemed to kick her sex drive into high gear. Just what she needed at a time like this.

An urgent thought distracted her from Olivia's softness and she stood straight up. Murray's voice rang loud and clear in her head. "Someone's coming. Are we done?"

"What? No. We have to get the wires," Olivia said.

Just then, the door beeped and a middle-aged man in a polo entered with a mop. Without thinking, Aerin closed her eyes, pressed her hands into Olivia's bare abdomen, stood on her tiptoes, and kissed her. The soft lips she pressed into were unyielding at first, surprised. She felt Olivia's confusion like a shock wave, rippling through both of their bodies, skin prickling beneath her fingers. She shouldn't have done this, even if it had caused the janitor to flee in embarrassment. It wasn't worth the complication and the questions Olivia would rightly ask later.

Just as she pulled away, she felt an unmistakable heat radiating from Olivia. Before she knew what was happening, they were kissing again. Olivia was leaning into her, wanting more than Aerin had realized. Then the air crackled and something shifted.

She was alone in the center of the storage room. A glint of something caught her eye and she turned toward the door. A liquid seeped in, clear and frothy. Suddenly the room smelled of energy, like standing beneath power lines. She backed away as far as she could, but the liquid crept toward her until she had to stand on a pile of boxes as it rose to her shoes. She cried out as she hit the back wall, as far from the liquid as she could get. Her heart pounded in her ears and the lights overhead flickered on and off. Aerin's skin sizzled as the fluid hit her ankles and she could tell it was the water from her dreams. It didn't make sense, though. She wasn't asleep. And this water, why would it be here? How could it get all the way down to New York City? And where was Olivia? Had she escaped?

"Olivia!" she screamed. "Murray?" There was no answer, only the gulping and sputtering of the toxic water as it slowly consumed the contents of the room. "No. No. Not again." Aerin panicked this time, though there weren't any dead bodies floating around her yet. It wouldn't matter if she saw them or not. If the water had risen this far up in the hospital, it had taken everyone already. It had taken Olivia. A surge of rage swept through her and she felt like throwing up. She was too late, it was over. She'd let those people down, again. She'd let Olivia down. Aerin dropped to her knees and let the water cover her thighs. It rose to her chest and she closed her eyes, ready to let herself float away when she heard a voice calling.

"Stand up. What are you doing?"

She lifted her face from the toxic liquid and blinked at the light above. Olivia stood above her, completely freaked out. "Get out of here. Get out now." Aerin gasped. When Olivia didn't move, she looked down. She was kneeling on all fours on a clean white linoleum floor, surrounded by medical equipment. She took Olivia's outstretched hand and pulled herself to a crouch.

"What. The. Fuck," Olivia said.

Aerin backed up against a shelf and hugged her legs, her eyes tearing up with relief and confusion. "I don't know. That's never happened to me before. I was here, there was this water…" The sensation of burning skin was a faint echo around her feet.

"Huh? I don't know what you're talking about. I'm talking about you kissing me. And making me kiss you back."

Aerin stared at her, finding no playfulness in her eyes. Not only did she not care about what had just happened to Aerin, she actually thought Aerin had made her feel desire. Which meant she hadn't wanted the kiss after all. Aerin felt like she'd been punched in the gut. She slowly stood, backing away toward the door. Olivia's face flushed angrily, and Aerin heard the yelling in her head. She wasn't sure which scenario was worse, having Olivia blame her for planting false feelings or thinking that she'd gotten Olivia killed. Once she'd dashed from the equipment room and stood safely on the other side of the door, she let the tears fall. Murray patted her arm and nodded.

"You did good, kid. And you should know that I heard every thought in her mind. You weren't in there making decisions for her." He looked at her with a fatherly affection that started to mend the cavity Olivia had just torn from her soul. "I just sent her a message to get the wires or whatever, and then we're out of here."

Aerin nodded numbly and leaned against the wall.

She barely registered footsteps coming up behind her. "Excuse me? I've got my mother in 318 and she needs a nurse," a middle-aged man said.

"She's busy, but let me alert one of her colleagues for you," Murray said. He closed his eyes and moments later, two nurses jogged over to the room.

"Wow, you've got such a handle on the mind influencing. I wish I could do that." Aerin wiped her face.

Murray chuckled. "You will. It's not going anywhere. You've got years to figure this out."

Aerin grimaced. As cool as her powers seemed to Zoe and Olivia, she would relinquish them in a second to go back to her old, boring life. The one she looked forward to living post-Josh. As Aerin contemplated the future Murray believed she would share with this alien, Olivia emerged from the supply room. Aerin didn't miss the slightly narrowed eyes as Olivia nodded in her direction.

"We're good to go." Olivia led the retreat. Nobody even looked at them twice as they left the hospital and caught a cab.

Back at the apartment, Olivia removed the taped equipment from herself, pointedly not asking Aerin for help.

"Here," she said curtly. "I'm going back to the hotel to get some rest. I guess I'll see you tomorrow morning."

Aerin wanted to stop her and explain that she wasn't the bad guy here, that she'd gladly give up whatever powers she had to see that spark in Olivia's eyes again. Instead, she let her leave like she had a decade and a half ago.

Chapter Forty-Four

Joshie, I'm so proud of you." Gladys Merkel pinched her son's shaved cheek. "She still insisting on keeping her own last name?" Josh glanced at Aerin with apology in his eyes.

"Mom, we've discussed this before. It's what she wants." He subconsciously reached his hand up to his tie and loosened the knot.

Aerin rolled her eyes. Gladys didn't even try to hide her disdain for Aerin's version of feminism. There weren't many liberal things you could do in Tireville and still be accepted by the community, but Aerin had figured out every single one. She refused to be a stay-at-home mom to the kids she assumed they'd be having and she would keep her own last name. She hadn't told Gladys the first part yet, and she planned to wait until the last possible minute. Her favorite, though, was going to college while Josh went to work for the family business. Not only did she plan to get her bachelor's, she'd also go back for her master's. Gladys really loved that one, and she enjoyed teasing Aerin about being an educated woman every chance she got. Nobody in Josh's family had gone to college, so Aerin was the odd duck out. She liked it that way. She'd rather be the intelligent outcast than conform to the standards of Tireville, even if she had chosen to stay.

"Hey, are you ready to get going?" Aerin asked. She felt the sweat drip down her back, moistening her shoulderless David's Bridal gown. "I need to take a shower."

Josh kissed his mom on the cheek and gave Aerin his hand as she stood. "My blushing bride. You look so sexy, baby."

Aerin kissed him on the lips and felt him start to get excited. She was tired and hot and didn't really want to consummate their marriage right now, but he would want to once they got back to the hotel. She'd do it for him, like she did most of the time. She didn't get a lot out of it, but at least he seemed happy with their lopsided sex life.

They drove down the road to the Sleep Inn, where most of the family was staying. Their house was only a half hour away. She'd give anything to sleep in her own bed, but that's not how things were done. She had to go back to the hotel and submit to a good fucking from her new husband.

Josh couldn't wait for her to shower. He started to undress her as soon as they got into the room. She didn't protest, just went with it. Her body responded to his out of habit. When he pushed himself into her, she moaned and closed her eyes. She always needed a little extra to come, either from her own hand or by fantasizing. She really wanted him to go down on her. After he had his orgasm, she pushed his head between her legs. Surely now that they were married, he'd do this one thing for her.

"Babe, you know I don't like to do that," he said. She sighed, defeated. He rolled off her and went to the bathroom. Alone, she closed her eyes again and touched herself. She didn't imagine Josh's hands or mouth on her, though. She imagined what she fantasized most of the time she was having sex, Olivia roughly touching her how she liked it, holding her all the way through, riding out her orgasm together.

The kind of release she got after imagining Olivia felt bittersweet. She was relaxed but upset. It reminded her how much she'd fucked up, how little she'd tried to make it work. Josh came back in and noticed her flushed cheeks. He didn't say anything, though, because deep down, he knew.

CHAPTER FORTY-FIVE

Olivia awakened in a terrible mood, unsure how much she'd slept, wishing she had the guts to just hop on a plane and leave. It was early, close to her normal wake-up time if she took into account the time difference. At least her body was sticking to its circadian rhythm. A surge of pleasure shot through her as she remembered the kiss, the one Aerin had made her want. Too tired to entertain any other possibilities right now, she imagined she hadn't enjoyed it as much as she did.

She checked out of the hotel before hailing a taxi, certain that no matter what happened today, she wouldn't end up back there again. She'd either be on a plane or, God forbid, somewhere with Aerin and Murray, stopping a bomb from killing a lot of people. In the cab she checked her email, shaking her head when she saw another one from Emmanuel. Just what she needed to compound the confusion in her life.

Dear Olivia,

I'm sorry that you don't want to see me. Mom and Dad are making me give the youth sermon at the Revival next weekend. I really don't want to go. I'm good at talking to people, but I hate the way everyone's eyes get all crazy when Dad shouts about Jesus and the fires of hell. Did he ever make you do the sermon?

I looked up pictures of your house online. It looks pretty big. School's almost over. Just another month and I can hang out with my friends. Dad's making me go to Bible camp this year. Usually it's just with a small group of people I like. This year we have to go backpacking and it's with like five other churches and I don't think we'll be with our friends.

I have a question to ask you. My best friend is named Evie and she's from Uganda. Her parents are really religious, so we hang out a lot at church stuff. She's really nice and funny. She's a year older than I am. Last week, she told me she might like girls. I don't want her to get kicked out of her house like you did. I don't think she has anywhere else to go. Mom and Dad would kill me if I let her stay here, if they knew. You know how they are. She wants to tell people, but I don't think it's safe. She doesn't have a girlfriend or anything, but she likes this girl at our church. I don't think the girl would be happy if she knew.

What should I do?

Emmanuel, your brother

Olivia let out a strangled sound. Her heart pounded in her throat and she had to cough to release the constriction. Her hands shook as she held the phone. Was this what a mental breakdown felt like? Now would be a good time for one. She felt Evie's pain as if it had happened to her yesterday. Confusion with a touch of self-hatred, desperation, devastation. Why couldn't she be more like everyone else? Why couldn't she have been born into a family who loved her more than they loved appearances? Her eyes welled up and she quickly wiped the tears away, blowing out a few deep breaths. She couldn't ignore her little brother, not when his friend's life was at stake. She wanted to believe that things had progressed beyond kicking gay kids out of their houses, but here he was telling her they hadn't. She typed a short response.

> *Dear Emmanuel,*
>
> *Please tell Evie I'm here if she wants to talk. If you or Evie are ever in trouble, you're welcome to come to my house. Although I don't necessarily want to get involved with the small-mindedness of Tireville again, I can't stand to see them do the same thing to either of you. I'm in New York right now, but I should be home soon if you need me.*
>
> *Olivia, your big sister*

The corners of her mouth curled into a small smile as she sent the email, even as a tear trailed down her cheek. Olivia felt helpless. She hated this loss of control, the break in her routine. She wanted to be the master of her own fate, but her life had cracked open, oozing out of its shell, and as hard as she tried to piece it back together, there would always be evidence of the fissures. Maybe she had kissed Aerin back. Maybe she was losing her mind.

They were nearing Murray's apartment building. A small group of little old ladies pushed carts of groceries past its front garden, alone even as they walked beside each other. She knew how they felt.

"This okay, miss?" The driver lifted his eyes to the rearview mirror and stared at her in a way that suggested a block from the building and across the street was going to have to be okay. She paid him and hopped out, jumping back as he took off again like he was entering a speedway. Jesus, she thought. Customer service clearly only applied while the customer was in the cab.

Reggie was at his shift again, and he nodded at her as she passed. "You have a good day now," he said.

Olivia dipped her head toward him. A few people milled around the lobby, one man on his cell phone having a heated conversation, and a family dressed in elaborate saris and sherwanis on their way to a wedding.

She didn't bother knocking or even announcing herself as she entered Murray's apartment. He slept on the couch and Aerin knelt beside the coffee table, stacking papers. When she looked around, Olivia understood why. Loose sheets littered the floors as if a tornado had torn through the place. Aerin continued to skim each page and place it in the pile without acknowledging Olivia. One moment went by and then another. She deserved to be ignored. She'd been an asshole yesterday.

"I'm sorry," she said softly, her voice cracking. Aerin briefly hesitated as she picked up a piece of paper with a strange landscape drawn on it, then she continued stacking as if she hadn't heard anything. Olivia walked to the coffee table and sat beside her. "I don't know what's going on anymore. I did kiss you last night. I'm sorry for saying otherwise."

Aerin stopped working but didn't look at her. She stared at the table, through the table, sadness etched on her brow. Aerin spoke softly. "There are some things more important than being with the person you love. But not many. And none of them are of this world." She took a paper out of the stack and placed it between them. "None of this could have happened without you and me together."

Olivia brought the sketch close to her face. She saw a vast expanse of water, a fountain of some kind, and three people standing on the edge, hands entwined, watching it. The details were incredible, down to the clothing. She looked down at the shirt she'd put on today, the same striped pattern as the taller, skinnier woman was wearing in the sketch. The other two figures were frighteningly similar to Aerin and Murray, same features and outfits. She glanced at Aerin, who nodded.

"Do you understand now?" Aerin asked. "Murray drew this in 1992. We were always going to find each other. You can ignore what's between us if you want, but he already knows how things turn out. This has already happened."

Olivia turned to look at her, goose bumps prickling her skin. Her eyes seemed to glow with a radiance that enveloped Olivia like gravity. Suddenly their histories were irrelevant. Their futures, too. Whatever the sketches showed seemed to be fixed in time. The scenes had already happened in Murray's mind. As for what would happen after the sketch she'd just seen, maybe Murray had drawn that as well, maybe it was already in that pile.

It didn't matter. We were always going to find each other, Olivia thought. She slowly closed her eyes, willing Aerin to kiss her again, hard, to remind her of the places she'd closed off, what it felt like to be fully herself again. When it didn't come after a moment, she opened them. Aerin stared past her. At first, she was disappointed that her feelings were not reciprocated after becoming vulnerable enough to acknowledge them. But she remembered what Aerin had said. Some things were more important than love, like whatever Aerin was seeing right now. Olivia had seen it, too. And it was definitely not of this world.

Murray stirred on the couch, yawning like he'd just had his best sleep in ninety years. "It's time to hear the message," he said.

Chapter Forty-Six

Aerin wasn't sure why Olivia was disappointed. She must have missed something, must have been in one of her trances.

She heard Murray behind her, shifting on the couch as the springs groaned under his slight body. "It's time to hear the message."

Aerin snapped back to reality. The message, yes, that's what they were waiting for. The reason Aerin had found Olivia and then Murray, so they could join together to access something important, something more than the sum of its parts. She'd seen bits of it through dreams, she'd taken trips with Murray to the other universe, she'd seen the drawings. They just needed one more unifying piece. Aerin could feel it. One more push in the right direction and they could save all those people. That's what this alien, or whatever it was, had come to do, after all. Help them keep people alive.

The only remaining question, whether it mattered or not, was why. She'd spent the last day with Murray contemplating why an alien civilization would bother keeping humans alive. So far, they'd only come up with a few explanations like benevolence or experimentation. Since they couldn't figure out which, or whether there might be a third, more sinister option, they had to go with benevolence. Any way it turned out, if her dreams and visions were correct, they'd be saving human lives.

Olivia looked at her hopefully and Aerin found herself smiling. She saw the possibility of another chance, one she'd hoped for over the last fifteen years.

"Can you hook us up to the machine?" Aerin asked. Olivia nodded without a hint of the hesitation she'd had since they'd arrived in New York. Perhaps even since Aerin had knocked on her door.

"Wait. I have one question for Murray before I do this," Olivia said suddenly. She used her phone to navigate to the university's computer science page and brought up a picture of Stanton. "Have you ever seen this person before?"

Murray scrunched his brow and blinked a few times. "No, I don't think so," he said.

Olivia stared at him for a moment, then nodded. Aerin shook her head in confusion. Of course Murray hadn't ever seen Stanton. When would that have happened? What a strange question for Olivia to ask.

She resumed applying the sensors to Aerin's head, electricity from her skin humming pleasantly against Aerin's hair. She wanted to reach out, take Olivia's hand, and hold it again, just like she had on the plane. She knew it would feel soft and vulnerable, warm with hope. There would be time for that later, though. After this entire operation was over, after they'd saved people.

She and Murray sat next to each other on the couch, their brains connected through a bunch of little wires feeding the EEG machine. Aerin took Murray's hand, its papery skin cool against hers. They both closed their eyes and let their brain waves speak.

After a while, Olivia said, "Huh. Okay. I think we're done."

Aerin opened her eyes and saw a strange look on Olivia's face. "We're done?" she asked.

Olivia nodded. "Yeah. There was some activity, then it went flat for a full thirty seconds. I've honestly never seen that before in a functional person. Or people. Let me send this to Stanton. Hopefully he has some time to translate this into some more creepy music that will give you two a vision or whatever happens when you hear it."

Aerin smiled to herself. Olivia was really cute when she pretended the methods that gave them answers were beneath her. A few minutes later, just as she'd mustered up enough courage to invite Olivia to sit beside her and maybe hold her hand, Olivia's phone buzzed.

"Wow, he really had nothing to do today. Got the file," she said.

Aerin took a deep breath and composed herself. "Okay, Murray, you ready?"

"Been ready since 1981," he said.

Olivia hit Play.

CHAPTER FORTY-SEVEN

A erin heard a voice through the darkness, a language that wasn't sound, but something closer to thought. It had a story this time, a story that Aerin and Murray needed to hear.

The Force, which is the basis for all things Rhuna, has always existed. Fourteen billion years ago, at the correct moment of potential, our Universe burst into being, a stew of particles bubbling up in the right combinations to create Consciousness. After a time, Consciousness created sentient beings, small creatures that looked like cubes and spheres and duplicated themselves at will. With their reproduction, Consciousness grew stronger. Then came our species, or rather the vessels we once inhabited. They look nothing like anything you've seen on your planet. Consciousness bound to all creatures that roamed Rhuna One.

Soon, our species realized that Consciousness does not like to be bound to bodies and furthermore, it does not like to be bound to a place. The part of Consciousness that inhabited Rhuna One since the beginning became restless and its creatures were running out of resources. Rhuna One was a dying planet, and in an effort to sustain itself throughout the Universe, Consciousness sent its highest level vessels, our species, to other planets. Our species had new homes, but Consciousness was still restless, still bound to bodies it yearned to escape.

Attempting to break free, Consciousness drew many members of our species living on Rhuna One together to unite. We know that as the first Unity Day. The energy should have released Consciousness from our bodies into the freedom of the Universe. But something was wrong. Some members of our species were too far from the truth and did not recognize the Consciousness in them. Instead, they were bound to their homes, to the planet, to the things they had acquired. They'd blocked the transfer of energy.

In time, a member of our species was born, one who united all creatures, great and small, and allowed them to look beyond themselves. We called the great uniter Rhunamian the First. Finally, Consciousness found a way to escape, during the second Unity Day. Each creature was surrounded by a glowing light, and as Consciousness left their bodies, they fell to become a part of Rhuna One once more.

Consciousness branched into the far reaches of the Universe, and with the energy it had gathered from millennia of reproduction, its sentience grew. It could see the future and past, not just the present. It saw that the future brought a slow, silent death to the Universe, one that would render Consciousness unable to exist any longer. Consciousness probed the Universe and found tiny rips in its fabric that led to distant places. Its only hope of survival was to find another Universe that had some time left, for all Universes are dying.

Consciousness sent out probes, pieces of itself, into the unknown. Each had just enough energy to explore and, if necessary, report back on the suitability of other planets, other Universes. The vast energy it took for them to leave the Universe, however, untethered them from Consciousness. Consciousness could see the future and knew that it would keep sending more and more energy through the rips, the portals from our world to yours, losing valuable pieces of itself each time. Eventually, there was no more energy to waste, so Consciousness waited for a signal it knew would come.

Our Universe is beginning to freeze. The Consciousness of the Rhuna Galaxy awaits word from your planet. The signal will be an almost insignificant energy shift at the portal through which we passed. Then we will know to come.

Chapter Forty-Eight

Aerin glanced back at Murray in the side-view mirror of their rental minivan. They were driving up 81 somewhere near Scranton, headed to Seneca Lake. Olivia thought she could make it in under four and a half hours, and with the way she worked with the little horsepower they had, Aerin believed her.

Murray hadn't seen any reason to worry about the content of the message and argued, via thought, that they ought to continue with their plan to somehow stop the bomb from killing the people in Aerin's dreams. Aerin was uncertain, though. She couldn't decipher the ultimate goal of the creature inside her. If they stopped this bomb, would she send a message back to the Rhuna Galaxy that it was okay to come on over and live with the humans? In the humans? The message chilled her, and she needed these four and a half hours to try and make sense of it.

She looked at Olivia, who stared expressionless at the road through her aviators. Aerin's gaze traced the edges of Olivia's mouth, around her curved jaw, and down her pale neck. She loved savoring this view. It was far from the frantic hormonal desire of her teenage years. Looking at Olivia this way was slow, thick like honey and intensely intimate. She knew Olivia now, her deepest thoughts, her motivations, the person she'd become. She was funny and sometimes crass, genius-level smart, and dependable. Olivia was the person she needed at this moment in her life and she knew Olivia felt the same way.

Olivia blushed under Aerin's scrutiny. "So, you're sure we're going to the right place?"

Aerin shrugged. "I'm not entirely sure, but Murray and I both feel it. We think there's a bomb that's going to be detonated under the lake sometime soon. I think we're supposed to stop it from doing as much destruction as it could." She hated lying to Olivia, but if she told her the truth now, she'd lose all the trust she'd worked to build. Better to fib now and deal with the fallout later. Eventually, it should even itself out.

"Do you know what time this bomb is supposed to be detonated and how?"

Aerin shook her head. "No, I don't." That part was true. Nothing in any of her visions, or Murray's drawings, or even the message, had given her any further information. Maybe they'd get there just in time? Now that she thought about it, maybe they were the ones who set it off.

"So, much like our little hospital field trip, we're vague on the details here." Olivia huffed.

Aerin glanced at Murray, who seemed to be lost in his thoughts. "Yeah, but that worked out fine, right?"

Olivia shook her head. "I don't know how you dragged me into this, but…" The sentence hung in the air between them.

"You're glad I did?"

Olivia looked at her, then turned back toward the road. "Would you have guessed that we'd be here now?"

Aerin chuckled, watching the highway roll under them, transfixed by the dotted lines disappearing beneath the van. "Honestly?"

"Yeah, tell me," Olivia said.

"I thought I'd be married to Josh with a bunch of kids, telling myself that living for the kids made me happy enough. Like, it didn't matter that I had this husband I didn't really care about because there were other fulfilling things. Isn't that sad? Every day of my marriage, I wished I'd married you."

She watched Olivia grip the wheel hard, then splay her fingers out. "Maybe when this is all over, maybe we can, you know, have dinner."

"Like a date?" Aerin asked, not quite sure she could trust the words she heard.

"What else would it be, a funeral?" Murray quipped from the back seat.

Olivia laughed and Aerin turned to reprimand him. He winked, then resumed staring out the window. Olivia's phone began to buzz and she reached for it, but Aerin got there first. "No cell phone use while driving. Do you want me to answer it?"

Olivia tried again to grab for it, but Aerin held it away. "Ugh, fine. Who is it?" Olivia asked.

"Looks like Jody. Want to talk to her?"

"Yeah, give me the phone." Olivia reached her hand out and waited.

Aerin moved farther toward the side window and answered. "Hello? This is Aerin. Olivia is driving. Do you want to talk to her?"

Jody laughed softly on the other end. "I do, but I'd love to talk to you, too. Olivia's not very good at gossip."

Aerin glanced at Olivia, who shot her several insistent glances. "Okay, let me give you to her first."

She waited patiently as Olivia and Jody talked about a number of things, some of which sounded like code words for other things. Aerin tried to listen in but couldn't keep track.

Mr. Piddles seemed to be doing fine, though he missed Olivia. He'd asked for Aerin once, though, which surprised both of them. The little parrot seemed to have deciphered what was going on between them.

"She wants to talk to you." Olivia narrowed her eyes. "No funny business."

Aerin lifted her hands in surrender. "Who, me? Yeah, let me talk to her."

"Hi, Jody, what's up?" she asked, as if she regularly spoke to Olivia's best friend on the phone.

"So, you two are just the cutest. Olivia will never tell me, but did you two kiss yet?"

"Um, yeah," Aerin said casually, certain Olivia would not want her divulging this information. Jody seemed like a safe person to tell. "Yes."

Jody's voice dropped to a whisper. "Did Olivia kiss you? Or was it the other way around?"

"Both." Aerin eyed Olivia to make sure she didn't understand the trajectory of conversation.

"Well, hallelujah. Thank you, Jesus. She's been pining after you for years. Sort of secretly, but it was no big secret to anyone who knows her."

"Oh," Aerin said. She was suddenly uncomfortable with that level of knowledge about Olivia's feelings. She didn't want to know about Olivia pining after her while she'd been figuring out how to get out of her failed marriage. She didn't want to hear any more secrets. "Hey, we're about to stop for a break. I'm going to let you go, okay?"

"You bet, and don't be a stranger, you hear?"

"Bye, Jody."

Olivia turned toward her. "We're stopping?"

"I have to pee."

Olivia's brow scrunched for a moment. "Oh, I guess I do, too," she said.

Aerin smiled to herself. She'd planted that thought and Olivia hadn't realized. She was getting better at this.

In the side mirror, she saw Murray practically roll his eyes.

CHAPTER FORTY-NINE

The closer they drove to Geneva, New York, the more
erratic Aerin's behavior became. It reminded Olivia of the
airport hotel after they'd landed in the city. Olivia watched
her bounce off the plastic walls of the van, changing the radio
station every few minutes and pointing out the mundane sights
along the road. It looked just like Indiana to Olivia, except
for the sparkling lakes and the rolling drumlins. They'd been
driving up Seneca Lake for twenty minutes and Olivia hated
the idea of stopping at the end. She wanted this magic, not the
horror a half hour away.

The road ran alongside vineyards that overlooked the
lake. Aerin pointed out some of the wineries that she and Zoe
had visited during their vacation. Olivia imagined a vacation
with Aerin in the south of France. Maybe Italy. Somewhere
quaint with wine that she and Aerin could sample before
heading back to their bed-and-breakfast for an afternoon nap,
then dining into the night. She could see it clearly, a future
together, with one small problem: Aerin wasn't fully Aerin
with that thing in her head.

"Do you think after whatever happens, happens, the thing
in your head will go away? I mean, what would it want with

you anymore? It just wants to save all these people, right?" Olivia asked.

Aerin looked at her thoughtfully from the passenger's seat. "I think so."

"I just want you to be back to normal," Olivia said quietly.

"Me too. But remember, you haven't known me without this thing in my head in fifteen years. How do you know that my normal is what you really want?"

Olivia shrugged. She didn't know how to answer that, she just knew. For one, she wanted a partner who wouldn't know every single thought in her head. She wanted someone who loved her and understood where she came from, who wouldn't hold her back. Aerin had been opening doors since they reconnected, showing Olivia new possibilities and different ways of seeing the world. The person she needed was Aerin and only Aerin. Not the alien inside her head. They drove in silence the rest of the way.

The expansive park lay just across the Geneva city line. The lake sparkled brilliantly before them, the tips of its tiny waves cresting and clashing in a mesmerizing dance. Olivia brought the van to a stop on the edge of the pavement. Aerin turned to her, brow knitted tightly, as if she wanted to say something painful.

"What is it?" Olivia asked, wishing she could kiss the worry away. After this was over, after Aerin had done who knew what, she would. And it would be Aerin through and through.

To her surprise, Aerin leaned over and pressed her lips to Olivia's. They were warm and yielding, and Olivia leaned in as Aerin pulled away.

"I'm so sorry." Aerin's lip quivered.

"I don't understand." Olivia turned back toward Murray, who stared out the window, pretending not to listen.

"If something happens to me, remember that I never stopped loving you. Never." Aerin squeezed her hand, kissed her knuckles, then turned away with eyes full of sorrow. She unbuckled her seat belt and got out with Murray following.

"Aerin, wait," Olivia said. She scrambled to undo her seat belt, but it stuck tight. The door handle was frozen, too. "Aerin, what is this?" she yelled. Nobody seemed to hear. They continued walking to the edge of the lake and stood there, looking out over its sparkling waters. "Jesus Christ, Aerin!" She banged on the window, trying to rip the seat belt off. It was no use, she was trapped inside the van.

To her right, another car pulled up and a young man stepped out. To her left, the same. She watched as dozens of cars deposited their passengers along the shoreline, each walking straight down to the water.

"Oh my God, we're all going to die," Olivia said to no one in particular. "Where's my fucking phone?" She fumbled the phone in her hands before she typed a shaky message to Jody. *Weird shit here. Aerin locked me in the car. Lots of people. Bomb might go off soon. No idea.*

Before she had time to send it, her phone went dark. Out of battery, dead. "Goddamnit, Aerin, I know you can hear me. What the fuck are you doing?" She thought it hard as she said it, sending all of her energy out to hopefully bring back a response. Instead, she just felt drained, like the phone. What was happening?

A glimpse of movement in the rearview mirror caught her eye. She turned and scanned the sparse trees, but there was nobody there. She was completely alone, witness to a bunch of possessed-looking people holding hands by a lake. Just then, dark clouds formed overhead and a flash of lightning drew her eyes upward. The ensuing crack of thunder wasn't that at all.

It came from inside the lake. A rumbling shook the vehicle, rippled the water left in a bottle next to her. The lake began to bubble far off in the distance, giant white globs pressing against the surface, bursting into the air. Olivia watched in horror as the middle of the lake formed a spout and flowed upward into the sky, higher than she could see. The water level lowered enough so that Aerin, Murray, and the rest of them walked out onto the glistening stones, still holding hands. Olivia tried her door again, but it wouldn't budge. She couldn't do anything but watch.

The fountain of water shooting into space began to slow until it just hung there, suspended in air for what seemed like an eternity. Olivia stared. It was beautiful, incredible, and it drew her in. Suddenly, gravity had it again, pulling the water down toward the basin. Once Olivia realized what gravity could do to that amount of water, it was too late. Millions of gallons of liquid crashed back into the lake at the same time. The deluge hit the van violently, rocking it back and forth.

Olivia let out a strangled scream. "No, Aerin, I'm coming." She prepared to yank the seat belt again, tear it off her body, but it gave easily. She tried the door and that opened, too. This wasn't good. Aerin wasn't controlling the van anymore. Outside was a warm misty mess of soaked grass, lake rocks everywhere, and nobody to be seen. She ran to the edge of the water, which fizzled with tiny opaque bubbles. Her shoes sank into the grass and oozed mud around them. The air felt static and smelled acrid. Frantically, she turned, hoping to find any of the people who were there, but she couldn't see anyone. She ran farther away from the water, praying Aerin would be there waiting for her, hoping she'd somehow got out before the water hit.

Fifty feet past the van, she saw a person sitting against a

tree trunk. She couldn't recognize them at first, but as she got closer, she recognized the outfit Aerin had been wearing that day.

"Thank God, thank God." Olivia ran over, her shoes making squishing noises as they took on water. "Aerin, please wake up. Please be okay." She felt for a pulse in her neck, but there wasn't one, and Aerin's lips were blue.

"Okay, okay." Olivia talked herself through the steps of CPR. She'd learned this before. She could do it. She had to.

A few chest compressions in, Aerin sputtered, gasping for air as Olivia turned her onto her side. She wheezed. "What happened?"

Olivia's lip trembled too much to speak, her throat constricted by imminent tears. She cried them into Aerin's dripping hair as she held her tightly. "Don't you fucking do that to me. Don't you do that. Oh God, I'm not letting you go again," she said. Aerin coughed, still catching her breath.

The sky, which had been clouded with mist, became clear and the brief storm dissipated. Olivia looked out over the lake again. There had been a lot of people there before the bomb blew. Now only one remained. No bodies bobbing up and down at the lake's surface. Olivia looked around her. The cars were gone, too, disappeared or washed away as if they'd never existed in the first place. The same hint of movement caught her eye again, and she followed it to a figure standing across a lawn under a large maple.

"Stanton?"

About the Author

Jane C. Esther is a librarian by day and a writer by night. Her idea of a good time involves a microscope, binoculars, trashy TV about the British royal family, or randomly singing Broadway show tunes. You can find her recounting the results of the latest scientific studies to whoever will listen and secretly transforming her house into an indoor vegetable farm. She lives in New England with her wife and cats.

Books Available From Bold Strokes Books

Dangerous Curves by Larkin Rose. When love waits at the finish line, dangerous curves are a risk worth taking. (978-1-63555-353-6)

Love to the Rescue by Radclyffe. Can two people who share a past really be strangers? (978-1-62639-973-0)

Love's Portrait by Anna Larner. When museum curator Molly Goode and benefactor Georgina Wright uncover a portrait's secret, public and private truths are exposed, and their deepening love hangs in the balance. (978-1-63555-057-3)

Model Behavior by MJ Williamz. Can one woman's instability shatter a new couple's dreams of happiness? (978-1-63555-379-6)

Pretending in Paradise by M. Ullrich. When travelwisdom.com assigns PR specialist Caroline Beckett and travel blogger Emma Morgan to cover a hot new couples retreat, they're forced to fake a relationship to secure a reservation. (978-1-63555-399-4)

Recipe for Love by Aurora Rey. Hannah Little doesn't have much use for fancy chefs or fancy restaurants, but when New York City chef Drew Davis comes to town, their attraction just might be a recipe for love. (978-1-63555-367-3)

The House by Eden Darry. After a vicious assault, Sadie, Fin, and their family retreat to a house they think is the perfect place to start over, until they realize not all is as it seems. (978-1-63555-395-6)

Uninvited by Jane C. Esther. When Aerin McLeary's body becomes host for an alien intent on invading Earth, she must work with researcher Olivia Ando to uncover the truth and save humankind. (978-1-63555-282-9)

Comrade Cowgirl by Yolanda Wallace. When cattle rancher Laramie Bowman accepts a lucrative job offer far from home, will her heart end up getting lost in translation? (978-1-63555-375-8)

Double Vision by Ellie Hart. When her cell phone rings, Giselle Cutler answers it—and finds herself speaking to a dead woman. (978-1-63555-385-7)

Inheritors of Chaos by Barbara Ann Wright. As factions splinter and reunite, will anyone survive the final showdown between gods and mortals on an alien world? (978-1-63555-294-2)

Love on Lavender Lane by Karis Walsh. Accompanied by the buzz of honeybees and the scent of lavender, Paige and Kassidy must find a way to compromise on their approach to business if they want to save Lavender Lane Farm—and find a way to make room for love along the way. (978-1-63555-286-7)

Spinning Tales by Brey Willows. When the fairy tale begins to unravel and villains are on the loose, will Maggie and Kody be able to spin a new tale? (978-1-63555-314-7)

The Do-Over by Georgia Beers. Bella Hunt has made a good life for herself and put the past behind her. But when the bane of her high school existence shows up for Bella's class on conflict resolution, the last thing they expect is to fall in love. (978-1-63555-393-2)

What Happens When by Samantha Boyette. For Molly Kennan, senior year is already an epic disaster, and falling for mysterious waitress Zia is about to make life a whole lot worse. (978-1-63555-408-3)

Wooing the Farmer by Jenny Frame. When fiercely independent modern socialite Penelope Huntingdon-Stewart and traditional country farmer Sam McQuade meet, trusting their hearts is harder than it looks. (978-1-63555-381-9)

Shut Up and Kiss Me by Julie Cannon. What better way to spend two weeks of hell in paradise than in the company of a hot, sexy woman? (978-1-163555-343-7)

Emily's Art and Soul by Joy Argento. When Emily meets Andi Marino she thinks she's found a new best friend, but Emily doesn't know that Andi is fast falling in love with her. Caught up in exploring her sexuality, will Emily see the only woman she needs is right in front of her? (978-1-163555-355-0)